The PINEDALE INCIDENT

The
PINEDALE
INCIDENT

by Larry Nemitz

Vidi Press
Whittier, California

COPYRIGHT

The Pinedale Incident
by Larry Nemitz

Copyright © 2011 by Larry Nemitz

ISBN: 978-1-934561-00-3

CONTACT AUTHOR
Larry Nemitz
Christian Discount Shop
165 Main Ave. South
Britt, Iowa 50423
1-641-843-9041
ChristianDiscountShop.com/

CONTACT PUBLISHER
Vidi Press
11721 Whittier Blvd. #203
Whittier, CA 90601
www.vidipress.com
800-409-7170

Contents

Acknowledgments

I would like to thank the following for their help and encouragement over the past fifteen years.

Bev Smith, Jessica Lynn, Dean Martinson, Mary Busha, Courtney Nieman, Editor Rachel Starr Thomson, Publisher Edie Glaser, and Cover Designer Lisa Hainline.

1

Is It You?

Christmas Eve, 1977

What had she said? Oh yes. Now he remembered. "And a blessed Christmas to you, Stan." Heavenly words from a once-worldly salesclerk as he purchased a gift and wished her a merry Christmas.

The young woman, Vicky Wills, was now manager and part-owner of the Pinedale Gift Shop, as well as a friend of Stanley's family. He couldn't help but note the change in her outlook from the first time they'd met.

For that matter, there was a change in the entire town of Pinedale. Yes, Christmas had meaning now, not only for Vicky and Pinedale, but also for Stanley and his family.

These were some of the thoughts drifting through Stanley Geraldson's mind as he drove the mile and a half to Westside Community Church.

The first snow of the season had started about an hour ago, and as it descended ever so gently past the

1

streetlights, it was especially beautiful. Usually the first snowfall was in early November, but this had been one of those warm winters. Stanley thought it appropriate that the first snow of the season should be on Christmas Eve. It had often been that way when he was growing up, a kid in southeastern Minnesota. He grinned. Or maybe he had just seen the movie White Christmas too many times. One of his childhood memories was of all the kids carrying water in buckets from the creek up to the top of the hill and letting it freeze as it ran down. They would slide down the ice on pieces of cardboard instead of sleds. "When I grow up" little Stanley used to say, "I'm going to move where there's a lot more snow."

Outside, the grassy terrain was already covered by a white blanket; and although the sidewalks were mostly wet, they would soon be covered, too. It must be a few degrees below freezing, Stan thought.

He was running late, for he had dropped off some gifts at a friend's and stayed too long. Stan promised Janet that he would check on their girls before the service started. He had driven Janet and the girls to church about forty-five minutes earlier, and while the girls were getting into their costumes, Janet warmed up with the choir in the basement below the sanctuary. Courtney, their eleven-year-old, would be Mary in the Nativity play. Stephanie, their nine-year-old, would be one of the angels. They were both nervous and excited. Stanley felt anxious for them.

Stanley joined Westside Community Church at the time of his marriage to Janet twelve years earlier. Its beautiful brick building with large, picturesque stones outlining the doors and windows certainly looked respectable. Light flowed out into the parking lot from the main building, which housed the sanctuary with its beautiful high ceiling and mahogany pews. Tall, narrow stained-glass windows along both sides of the sanctuary depicted the stories of Christianity: to the right, the story of Easter; to the left, the Christmas story with the angel Gabriel proclaiming to Mary the birth of the Savior.

As he parked his car, Stanley could hear music drifting through the snowy air. The Easter service was more important on the church calendar, but the Christmas Eve service was the most beautiful of the year. A violin and piano, followed by a horns and drums started the service. The children's Nativity play followed leading into angelic hymns sung by the choir and the congregation. After the reading of the Christmas story from the Bible, there would be a short, uplifting sermon. Last, and best of all, the lights would be turned off. By the flickering light of the candles on the altar and on the ends of the pews, everyone would sing "Silent Night." Among the adults, hardly a dry eye in the congregation could be found. As got out of his car, he smiled big and boldly thinking about what a beautiful end the service would be to a perfect night.

It was almost seven, the service was about to begin, and the snow was falling a little more heavily. Stan hurried up the sidewalk to the side entrance. A man's footsteps behind him startled him—he thought he'd be the last arrival. A gust of wind swirled around the entry area. Stan opened the door as he turned to greet the man behind him with a hearty "Merry Christ—"

The greeting wouldn't come out. It all came back to him, engulfing his mind as if the incident had happened only yesterday. *John?* He couldn't say the name, but he thought it. His knees began to buckle and so he held the door handle tightly for fear of collapsing onto the sidewalk.

The man looked at him with deep concern, asking kindly. "Are you all right?"

Stan shook his head to clear the voice away. It wasn't John. He'd been mistaken.

"Do you need help?" the man persisted.

A cold, heavy sweat broke out over Stanley's entire body. He could feel the flow of perspiration from under his arms trickling down his sides.

"Oh . . . ah . . . yes," he muttered. "I'll be fine; you just startled me. I thought you were someone I knew."

Stan brushed himself off, assuring the stranger once again that he was all right. He let the man go in ahead of him.

As he stood thinking of those days three years ago, he wondered if the events really could have taken place. They had been the most wonderful, yet the most mysterious and stirring days of his life.

And that was the Christmas Eve when they didn't sing "Silent Night"

2

THE GREAT DIVIDE

Summer, 1962

The early June evening felt hot, muggy, and full of promise as Stanley Geraldson crossed over Worth Street in his old Ford beater and wound his way through the streets of the east side of Pinedale. The elevation descended as he drove down to the Branch River, which meandered its way through Pinedale's east side and eventually entered into the Mississippi River just south of Saint Paul.

Twenty-four years old and newly graduated from the University of Minnesota, Stanley was ready, and in his opinion more than able, to take hold of his share of the riches of the world. Owning a new home in Westside Pinedale overlooking rolling hills covered with abundant maple, birch, blue spruce, and northern pine trees became the first of many goals. The wooded surroundings were beautiful year-round; but in the fall, the splendors of green, gold, and red could not be matched by any natural phenomenon. Every time he viewed the live painting, he thought that God must be real; but then, he couldn't understand how such a beautifully creative God would allow so much violence and pain in the world.

It's too bad that this area of Pinedale has so many areas in such a rundown condition, Stanley thought, wrinkling his nose as he pulled into a gas station. Even in this Wisconsin tourist town of only 12,000 people, two classes lived side by side. What the townsfolk called the "less fortunate" and "summer workers" dwelt here on the east side, their less-than-glamorous surroundings made up of several gas stations, half a dozen rundown bars—some featuring nude dancers—and two greasy, hole-in-the-wall restaurants, one of which served the best cheeseburgers in the upper Midwest.

Stanley surveyed the street as the attendant pumped the gas and checked the oil. A pawnshop called Lefties and a small newsstand that sold pornography decorated Worth Street directly across from him. But the most notorious business on the east side stood the Pinedale Pool Hall, just up the road and already flashing neon signs in the early evening. Stanley snickered to himself as he watched cars pulling in. The pool hall was most famous for what went on upstairs. When you wanted "upstairs action" you could ask to play pool on table four. Those were the magic words: table four, a table upstairs with a mattress on top of it.

The local police raided the pool hall once or twice a year, giving the girls a one-way bus ticket to Minneapolis or Chicago. Then they fined the owner. But within a few weeks, new girls arrived.

Gambling went on in the east side, too—a lot of it—Las Vegas-style with added features: plenty of poker rooms, pull-tabs, craps, and pinball machines that paid off. More than enough slot machines (in those days called "one-armed bandits") lined the walls, and bookies took bets for almost any sporting event. While the pool hall got raided once in a while, the authorities mostly overlooked the gambling. With all this activity, some of the townspeople said that Worth Street was the dividing line between heaven and hell. Others called the east side "Satan's Den," or just "Little Vegas."

Stanley began to smell the muggy air mixed with gas fumes and drunks who had just lost their lunch. He moved his eyes from Worth Street to the west, up where the air was cleaner and the trees beckoned him to come nearer. His job already showed promise of being good to him. *I'll be moving up to "heaven" soon,* he beckoned back. *With Janet.*

Janet Swartz was Stanley's future bride, although she didn't know it yet. They had only dated twice, but he loved her so much he could hardly stand it. She also worked at Kellene Industries, as the receptionist and sometime secretary for the company owner, Barrett Kellene. Janet was tall for a girl, five foot-ten, and *very good looking* Stanley thought. She was so intelligent and so confident with such a wry sense of humor that she turned Stan into a neurotic mess. Stan's desk was only a few feet from hers, and when the guys at work would hover around her, he got both angry and fearful that he might lose her. He got a sick feeling in the pit of his stomach whenever he thought about her, and that was all the time. He had trouble sleeping and he didn't feel like eating.

As the attendant finished cleaning the windows, Stan jumped back into the car and rehearsed the lines he would say that night on their third date. He reviewed what he would wear, say, and be: smooth, confident, and respectful. Oh, and saying the right things about God and church and things like that. Janet was very religious, going to church every Sunday, singing in the choir, visiting the elderly at rest homes and the sick at the local hospital. She was different from other girls, that was the truth. She wasn't afraid of the boss either, like most of the office staff. She was stable, that's it—it was her stability that Stan liked most.

He threw his car into gear and roared up the road toward the apartment where he was biding time until he could afford to move. He thought, with his hard work and Janet's being tried-and-true, their marriage might just last. That is, if he could move fast enough to win her heart before she moved on to a full-time job in New York in late September.

That evening, a nervous, tongue-tied Stan apologized to Janet as he stopped the car to check on a tire that seemed low. "I'll only be a moment," he assured as one polished shoe crunched down on the gravel by the side of the highway. Stan felt confident and protective just as he practiced. But then, halfway out, the car lurched forward, knocking Stan to the ground. By the time he scrambled back on his feet, the car, with a very surprised girlfriend in the passenger seat, drove itself toward midtown at about fifteen miles per hour. "Hey!" Stan yelled, kicking up gravel as he tore down the street after the runaway Impala. He could feel his face flaming as he waved his arms and shouted, "Stop the car!"

Janet moved over into the driver's seat and brought Stan's car to a stop, placing the gear in park rather than drive as Stan left it. Panting, Stanley caught up. Janet stuck her head out the driver's window: "Want a ride, good looking? Or do ya wanna jog some more?"

Stan wished he could die on the spot. "Just move over," he said. "I'll drive now." He cleared his throat as he adjusted the rearview mirror and tried to stop his hands from shaking. He couldn't even look at her. The best he could do was say, as calmly as possible, "Ya know, someday we'll laugh about this."

But Janet, biting her lip, replied, "Sorry, Stan, I don't think I can wait." She put her head against the passenger window. "That has to be the funniest thing I've ever seen, for sure." Her soft giggle built to loud, roaring laughter. Finally, Stan started laughing too. They laughed so hard tears fell from their eyes, and Stanley knew he would never be uncomfortable with her again. He wanted to spend the rest of his life with this wonderful girl.

As their laughter died down and they wiped their eyes, Stan heard his voice say something like, *Will you marry me, Janet?* It didn't come out of the mouth, but it was about to. Stanley winced. *Don't, don't do it, don't do it,* he told himself. But he carried on anyway.

"Janet, I know it's too soon. After all, we've only known each other about three weeks. Well, I think you know that I'm in love with you. I mean, by the dumb things I've been doing, the things I've said."

He shifted in his seat and looked her full in the face. She was listening, her eyes still watery from laughter. "I never, ever thought I could love anyone as much as I love you. Janet, will you marry me?"

Her voice seemed so soft and warm. "Stanley . . . it's much too soon to talk about marriage. I'll think about it. Ask me again in a few months, then maybe."

Stanley asked two weeks later, and two weeks after that, and finally she said yes. Janet willingly canceled her plans to move to New York. "After all," she told Stan, "I have what every women wants: a good, hardworking man with ambitious plans." Only a week after Janet said yes, Stanley got a raise and knew that living in heaven on the Westside with his bride would soon be a reality.

3

BARELY HONEST JOHN

John Nelson stared out the window of his used-car lot which he affectionately named Fairly Honest John's, wishing something interesting would happen. It had been a slow, lonely morning and afternoon, with only two tire kickers all day. Not that he could complain—business, overall, had been good. Just yesterday he learned that his banker approved his loan to buy three acres still on the east side of Worth Street, but much closer to the downtown area. That would certainly be a boon to his business.

Pondering his expansion, John noticed a car pull up to his office window: *a '50 Ford, a real bomb*—dark pink, or maybe it was a badly-faded maroon. It looked like it had been smeared with house paint by five-year-olds. *This guy could certainly use a new car.*

The driver started looking through the lot while John started sizing him up: early twenties, probably two or three years younger than himself. Good-looking in a rugged sort of way. Height, just under six foot. Dark brown hair, square jaw, and medium build. John had seen him several times before, mostly at the nightclubs and bars on Worth Street. He remembered asking someone what his name was and where he worked, but the name escaped him. He did remember that he worked at Kellene Manufacturing and was a native of Minnesota. *Probably a Minnesota Gopher and Viking fan,* John thought. With Pinedale being so close to the Twin Cites, there were too many of those people around already.

John pushed back his chair and headed for the office door. He wondered if he could unload one of his demolition models. Although he always felt guilty whenever he sold one, John had been lucky so far. He only had to settle with a couple of customers who found out that their cars had been formerly totaled. John grimaced. Maybe he wouldn't try that again.

In fact, lately he'd been thinking that he would clean up his act. If he was going to be successful in the used-car business, he would need a better reputation for honesty. In the future, he would better explain the major problems with the cars he was selling. Better yet, in the future, he wouldn't purchase cars that had been in major accidents or even natural disasters like floods and tornadoes. *When I get my new lot on Worth Street,* he promised himself, *I'm going to start a more truthful advertising campaign.*

His eyes strayed to the end of the parking lot where some of the demolition cars sat, spruced up and impressive-looking. He had to do *something* with them, didn't he? For now he was still on the east side, out in the sticks. *Until I move, it's buyer beware.*

John strolled over to the newcomer. "Hi, I'm John Nelson. Can I show you some fine, used cars?"

He cringed at the insincerity in his own voice. At least he didn't sound like he did in his TV commercials. "Hi,

I'm Fairly Honest John, and do I have a gerrr-great car for you today!"

"Yes," the young man replied. "I'm Stanley Geraldson, and I've just moved to Pinedale. I thought I'd better get rid of my Minnesota car—doesn't seem like a healthy thing to drive around Wisconsin Badger country, if you know what I mean." He laughed. "If you can't tell, those colors are supposed to be maroon and gold. I'm looking for something a little newer, maybe a '59 or '60 model."

"I have several that might interest you," John said, raising an eyebrow. *I'll bet there's an interesting story behind that paint job.*

"I hear you can get a pretty good deal here," Stanley said as John showed him around the lot. "I've heard some good things about you."

Well, that's being overly polite, John thought, but he kept his sarcasm to himself. "The townspeople all know me. I've lived in Pinedale all my life, and you've probably seen or heard some of my radio and television commercials." He laughed. "Everyone else has."

They chatted for a few minutes, and then John said, "Ya know, Stan—is it all right if I call you Stan?"

"Yes, that would be fine."

"I'd like to hear the story behind that '50 Ford. I mean, the paint job."

Stanley laughed. "Rosy? She served me well over four years of college. Many a cold winter morning in Minneapolis, at the dorm, Rosy was the only car that would start. I'd get my jumper cables out of the trunk and get all the guys' cars started at five dollars a crank. I named her Rosy in my sophomore year after the guys in my dorm, without my knowing, painted her maroon with gold trim in honor of the Minnesota homecoming football game." Stanley grinned, clearly enjoying the memories. "I was furious at first, but

13

it seemed that every girl on campus wanted to ride in her. I made a fortune renting it out to my dorm buddies when I had to study. Because of them, the backseat became notoriously known as 'Planker's Paradise.'"

Stan smiled and laid a proud hand on the Ford's trunk. "Seems to me she ought to be put on a pedestal back at the U in honor of her faithful service, but there you go. Times change and I need a newer car."

The men chatted a while longer, covering sports, politics, and world problems. They discovered they shared opinions on many subjects. And in the meantime, John sold Stanley a car.

Stan started to leave when John called out, "Oh, ah, one more thing: the transmission needs to be worked on. Should cost around two hundred fifty dollars. You get that fixed and I'll pay half, and you'll have yourself one fine automobile."

Stan agreed to get the work done and thanked John for his candor. John watched as Stanley drove out of his used-car lot, wondering why he had told him about the transmission problems. After all, he had put a special additive in the transmission that would cover up the problem for about fifty miles. He knew the reason: he felt guilty—but why? Why did he feel guilty when others cheated their customers all the time and never felt anything?

For one thing, he told himself, *I like Stanley. In fact, the next time I see him at one of the watering holes, I'll buy the guy a drink.*

Satisfied, John turned and headed back into his office and called his buddy at the only auto-repair shop in town that worked on transmissions. He would get a nice kickback for the work on Stan's car.

4

OH NO. NOT MARRAIGE

Fall, 1962

Stan sat at his desk contemplating the events of the last few months. The love of his life was going to be his bride, and he had never before been so happy and contented. The anguish he had felt before was gone, and since Janet now wore his engagement ring, the guys at the office weren't hanging around her desk as much.

The wedding would be in August, six months away. Stan thought it seemed like forever. If he could have his way, it would be this weekend. He looked over at Janet, who was busy typing. As if she could sense him, she looked up and met his eyes. They both smiled. Stan ducked his head and got back to work, savoring the sense of her nearness but knowing that he needed to quit daydreaming. Mr. Kellene stopped by Stan's desk that morning, and after going over some inventory figures, casually remarked, "I'm glad you two are engaged; maybe now I can get some work out of you."

Janet paused in her typing to file a couple of letters. As much as she enjoyed having her tall, square-jawed fiancé across the office, she wondered if she had made the right decision. Despite the fact that she picked him out almost the first day he joined the company, she wasn't sure that she loved Stanley, at least not yet. But she was comfortable with Stan, and he would make a good husband. The boss liked him, and he was almost guaranteed to climb the corporate ladder rapidly. They would both work until their first child was born; then she would be a home mom and wife. They were already saving for that new home on the west side of Worth Street.

She allowed herself a wry smile as she thought of her mother's advice—advice she intended to heed. "Most men worth marrying only like to sleep over for a night or two, and then they're gone. So keep them out of your bed until the honeymoon, otherwise there might not be a wedding."

Janet knew enough about men to realize that her mother was right. She was sure that Stanley thought she was a virgin and hoped that *almost* would be good enough. She blushed as she sat back behind her typewriter and realized that Stanley was smiling at her again.

Yes, she was doing the right thing. She was going to marry Stanley, and they would go far together.

A crisp, gorgeous fall morning greeted the men at the first tee. John breathed the invigorating air as he waited for Stanley. The two had become great friends and played golf or tennis several times a week; they even double-dated occasionally—Stanley bringing Janet, and John bringing whatever girl he was dating at the time. No girl seemed to last more than a few months.

After they both bogged the first hole, Stan sensed the time was right to ask, "Janet and I have finally set the date for our wedding, and I was wondering if you would like to be my best man?"

John's sandy brown eyebrows rose. "I'd love . . . of course, I'll . . . what I'm trying to say is, it would be an honor to be your best man. When's the big day?"

"She says next summer. But if I had my way, we would elope tomorrow."

"You know, you're lucky you met her first. If I ever meet a girl like Janet, maybe even I'll get married."

Truth was that John had seen Janet several times over the last few years. He did see something special in her but never asked her out. *Maybe it's her religious life and how she seems to be a little above my class*, John thought.

Stan cleared his throat. "John, why haven't you married? I've met some of the girls you've dated, and I must say, there were several that Janet and I thought would make a great wife for you."

"Well . . . ah . . . I'm not sure. It will happen someday, I suppose."

John frowned. Memories of his own father—the divorce when John was twelve, the death from cancer only two years later—marred the beauty of the morning.

"Stan, you still have honors. Hit the ball, will ya, and let's talk about something else."

They hardly said a word to each other for the next several holes, and Stanley never again brought up the subject of why John hadn't married.

Being that it was Sunday morning, like every golf game day, they held a mock church service on the ninth green. "Amen," John said taking his ball out of the hole. Stanley, missing his short putt blurted an "aw—?&!#." Clearing his throat, Stanley continued, "About our golf game—I promised Janet that I would start going to church with her on Sundays. I'm sorry. You know I'd rather be out here with you on the course than in church with all those hypocrites anytime."

John smiled. "Don't worry about it. I understand. Anyway, I could use the extra sleep on Sunday mornings."

Alone, after Stanley departed, John sat in his car overlooking the golf course. He was happy for Stan and Janet, but couldn't help comparing his own personal life (or lack of it) with Stan's. Why *hadn't* he married? He wasn't really sure. All he knew was that he wasn't going to stay down forever. He and Fairly Honest John's would leave the east side of town and make a name for themselves—one way or another.

About a year after Stan and John met, John bought his three acres on the south end of Worth Street. He had to build on the east side of the street, though, as Pinedale zoning laws forbade his type of business on the west side. It didn't matter. There he found even more success, so much so that he believed the time arrived to build his dream house on the west side of town.

5

WHO NEEDS A PSYCHOLOGIST

Winter, 1964

A year and half after Stanley and Janet married, their first child was born—Courtney. John agreed to be her godfather and both of the men tried to get together at least once a week, and they did pretty well until Stephanie was born two years later.

Courtney and Stephanie loved their honorary "Uncle John," but by the time Courtney had her fifth birthday, they were seeing very little of him. Janet and Stanley planned to have him over for dinner once or twice a month, but as it turned out, he only came once every other month. With John's increasing business and their growing schedules, they both knew they would have little time for all the things they used to do. Stanley missed their Sunday golf games, but he felt that going to church with his family was more important—just one of the sacrifices men have to make when they get married.

19

Everything seemed to be going great for John. He was a successful businessman with a beautiful new home on the right side of town. He wore the best clothes, vacationed part of the winter in Hawaii, and always drove expensive new cars. John seemed to be enjoying "the good life."

And on that infamous day, no one else heard the conversation. No one else had to. "Boss, do you want me to hold any calls that come in?" asked John's assistant.

"Yes, Lisa," was all he said. John sat with his elbows resting on the polished mahogany desk and head in his hands as Lisa ushered in Homer, the loan officer, and Mr. Bridges, the bank president.

"Hi John." Said Homer. Both men stretching out their hand. John laid his on his desk. "We're sorry it has to come to this, John," Homer said as the men sat down. "You're hopelessly behind in all your payments to us. We really have no choice in the matter. Mr. Bridges and I have decided that it's time to close your business down."

"If you can just give me—" John started, but Homer held up a hand and signaled him to be quiet. "The owners of the radio and television stations came in to see us, and they're very worried about the money you owe them."

Mr. Bridges leaned forward and pushed a stack of papers across the desk. "Just sign these papers that allow us to auction off all your cars and the lot. You have ninety days to sell your house or we'll have to auction that off as well. The bank debt will be paid off first, then your other creditors. If any funds are left over, of course, they will be yours."

John could barely breathe. He knew this was coming—some day, though he didn't know how cold-blooded it would be. A ton of bricks seemed to rest on his chest.

"Where do I sign?" was all that he asked.

Pointing to the spot, the bank president said, "We'll need all the cash and checks that are here in the office. We'll give you a deposit receipt for those funds. You have one hour to pack up your personal things and vacate the property. Homer will wait in his car while you pack, and when you leave, you can give him the keys. He will put up all the auction signs and rope off the two entrances to the lot."

Mr. Bridges' face softened as he took in John's expression. "John, we're sorry that we have to do this. It's a banker's nightmare to have to foreclose on someone."

A few moments later, John stood at the window, watching Mr. Bridges drive off. He saw Homer get into his car where he would wait to make sure John didn't take anything other than his personal belongings. He turned to Lisa and said, "I'm sorry, Lisa . . . I guess your job . . ."

"Boss, you okay?"

Was he? His chest was tightening, and he could hardly gasp out the words to answer her. "Call ambulance . . . can't breathe," was all John could get out as he sat down, trying desperately to get some air into his lungs. *What is happening to me? How could so much go wrong all at once?*

The ambulance rushed John to the hospital, where he was diagnosed with a severe anxiety attack. "This reaction is normal during moments of high stress." The doctor said. "To help you cope, here's a prescription to relax you, and a few names of psychologists that I highly recommend."

Who needs a psychologist! John thought as the next couple of weeks blurred by. The bank auctioned all the cars and John sold his beautiful home. Fortunately, he had enough money left over to buy a commercial building housing a small gift shop on the east side of Worth Street. A modest apartment above the shop became his new home.

The night he settled in, John sat in the living room of his new apartment clutching a pillow in his arms as the tears rolled down his checks. *How did this get so out of control?* He knew the answer—he just didn't want to open his eyes to it. Nobody but the bank knew about the huge debt he had accumulated. If his accountant told him the truth about his financial problems, he would just change accountants. Anyway, the friendly bankers kept lending him more and more money, so he believed everything must be okay. But one day, they said, "no more." And another day the radio and television stations stopped selling him time. But John covered the facts with wishful thinking, *They'll change their mind when they realize how much they need me.*

That's what he used to think. *I'm a failure.* John now said to himself over and over. *Dad was right. I'll never amount to anything.* It was a terrible thought, but he was glad that his father was dead—at least he couldn't say, "I told you so" or hear about it in the town square. His near bankruptcy and move to the east side was the talk of every drunk on Worth Street and quite a few notables in the rolling hills in the west. He was humiliated.

John walked into the bedroom and to the window, where he looked down on the parking lot at the back of his building. It was early evening and the lot was nearly half full with customers of the bars and strip joints along Davis Avenue Their back doors led to the same parking lot that served his gift shop.

Straight across from John's window on Davis Avenue was the Pinedale Pool Hall where most of the traffic, mostly men, went. John could see the lights of the second floor where table four stood. He found a strange solace in looking down on the desperate men entering the building. He had never played pool on table four. Why would anyone pay twenty-five dollars when so many girls were willing to give it away?

As the night wore on, John sat on the couch. Garish lights from Little Vegas shone in. Brawls ricocheted around the parking lot until three in the morning. He had no desire to join them that night. He just wondered what God thought about all the drinking, gambling, and sex. John pulled himself off the couch, walked over to the bed, and dropped to his knees. He wasn't sure why he did it. He just knew he needed some kind of help.

"Oh God, help me." He swallowed hard, trying to keep his voice from cracking. "I don't know what to do; please help me. I'm so miserable I just want to die."

6

THAT GOOD OL' TIME RELIGION

Stanley and Janet noticed, offhandedly, that John wasn't on the radio anymore, but they never could have dreamed why.

"Janet!" Stan yelled as he came home. "Janet!"

"What Stan? What's wrong? Is the girls? What happened?"

"No, no. I just drove by John's lot, and ... well, it's all taped up with auction signs all over the place."

"No. That can't be."

"Yes it is. And I saw Mr. Bridges, the bank owner walking the lot."

"Oh no. Well that explains a lot, doesn't it." Janet said. "We have to invite John over for dinner right away."

"I will right now. But let's not tell him that we know. Let him tell us."

"You're probably right. Okay. I hope he comes."

Eyeing John's expressions, John appeared to Stan to be relaxed. Now that his financial burdens were behind him, Stan believed that a great weight had been lifted from John but not a word about it had been discussed at dinner. Courtney, now five, and Stephanie, three wouldn't go to bed until he read them a story, heard their prayers, and tucked them in. Although John was shy around most strangers, he wasn't at all shy with children. In fact, his face lit up whenever children came near him. Still watching him, Stanley wondered anew how he could have done all those commercials on television and yet be so reserved with adults.

Stanley and Janet determined that tonight had been great therapy for John. The three of them talked about the girls and how they had grown as Janet served coffee and cake. Finally, Stan broke the silence, "I've heard about your problems and am very concerned about you, John." Stanley wanted to word it just right. He didn't want John to think they were offering him a loan.

"Everything is okay now," John said. "I appreciate your concern; I just spent too much money and played golf instead of tending to business." Abruptly, he changed the subject. "Lately, I have been thinking a great deal about religion. Would you tell me about your church? As you know, I've only been there once, and that was for your wedding."

"We're very involved in our church," Janet said. "In fact, Stan is on the church board, and I sing in the choir, and we're both deacons." Seeing the blank look on John's face, she explained, "It's a deacon's job to visit hospitals and rest homes and participate in other areas of the church. It's the least we can do as a good Christian family."

"Yeah," Stan added, "the girls go to Sunday school every week and say their prayers every night." He laughed. "I can't say I don't miss the golf course; but by and large, religion has been a good thing for us."

"What about God?" John asked, his tone more intense than was comfortable for Stan. "Do you ever think about God and the possibility that there's a heaven and hell?"

"Of course we believe in God," Stan said, "and we're trying to do the best we can. If there is a heaven, we'll certainly be there someday. And as for hell, I don't believe in it."

John raised an eyebrow. "That's interesting—you don't believe in hell? Hope you're right."

Stan laughed again. "Look, not all Christians are the same. There might be a hell, I suppose—for Hitler, and that guy who crucified Christ, Pontius the pilot, or whatever his name is. You know, people like that." He shrugged. "It makes sense."

"I haven't been inside a church in many years, except for weddings and funerals. Anyway, I'm thinking about starting to go again, and Westside Church seems as good as any. I met your pastor at your wedding, I think. He seemed a little stuffy and overeducated, but aren't they all?"

Stanley and Janet both laughed. Janet set down her coffee cup and laid her hand on Stanley's knee.

"John, I think going to church is a wonderful step for you. Would you join us this Sunday? Stan and I would love to have you, and the girls will be very excited."

"Yes, and we'll go out for lunch afterward," added Stan. "Is it all right if we pick you up at 9:45?"

"That sounds great," John said as they continued talking about the kids and school and life until John rose from his chair and turned to Janet and Stan, "Well, I better get going. Lots to do. Thank you both for dinner and your kindness. Now I know what friends are for."

Stan and Janet stood in their doorway and watched John drive off, satisfied that they were doing their part to help their friend get back on his feet.

John did attend church with the Geraldson family the following Sunday, and a few months later he became a member of Westside Community Church. Within the next two years, he had joined the choir, become a deacon, and even started teaching Sunday school. He was an exemplary member, and there wasn't anything he wouldn't do for his new church, even though he lived on the east side.

As one might guess, Westside Church got its name from being on the west side of Worth Street, or as many would say, "the right side." It was an affluent church, yet almost a third of the members, including Stanley's family, were from the east side. Pastor Whitehearst held tight oversight on every aspect of the church.

For one thing, he either handpicked or had final approval over everyone from the assistant Sunday school teacher to the official board members, and he made sure no more than one or two board members came from the east side of town. But even with Pastor Whitehearst's strict rule, Westside Church was for the most part a comfortable, friendly church.

7

I'LL DO IT

A beautiful spring day enveloped the service as Pastor Reginald Whitehearst looked out over the congregation from his cushioned chair, contemplating his twelve years of service at Westside Church. He remembered his first year: it had been difficult, the church full of strife and petty jealousies. Through cunning maneuverings and endless meetings, he had worked through all the discord and bickering. He wasn't going to repeat the mistakes of the past. He had pastored his first church in his home state of Connecticut. After three years of controversy and opposition, he had resigned his duties in utter disgust and exhaustion. He returned to Yale to get his doctorate in psychology in order to acquire knowledge of why people act the way they do. He could use that knowledge to better handle and direct difficult people to his way of thinking.

Pastor Whitehearst came to Westside Church in 1958 at the age of twenty-nine with his wife Helen and their two-year-old son, ready to put his newly attained education to work. For he was going to take on a northern tourist-town church in trouble. And in fact, in just three years, Westside Church became one of Pinedale's most prominent and fastest-growing congregations.

"Pastor Whitehearst is daydreaming again," Stanley whispered to Janet from their usual pew about ten rows from the front.

Janet elbowed Stanley. "Quiet, Stan."

The choir had stopped singing, and Stanley wondered how long before Pastor realized it.

Stanley eyed his watch—thirty-two seconds—when Pastor Whitehearst rose from his chair and walked to the lectern. It became a game for Stanley. He often thought of recording the gaps for posterity but was deathly afraid of Pastor finding out.

As Pastor read the Scripture of the day, Stanley started to daydream, too. right on cue. At first, Stanley hadn't enjoyed attending church, but it wasn't so bad now. It was good for Janet and the girls, and after he got into the habit of going, it was okay for him, too. Besides, as far as churches went, Westside was the least offensive of the lot. Pastor Whitehearst's sermons never lasted longer than twenty minutes, and the entire service was usually forty-five to fifty minutes long—except at Christmas and Easter. They were always home in plenty of time for the noon-time football game.

Stanley's eyes wandered across the pews to where John Nelson sat, taking notes on today's topic—good community and church standing. Stan liked the fact that Pastor didn't talk about religion like those self-righteous, born-again losers who preached on television. In fact, he would say, "Our Lord," or "Christ," but very seldom "Jesus." The terminology kept everything formal and distant, just how Stan liked it.

When Pastor said something about contributing to worthy causes, Stan almost snorted out loud, but Janet's elbow kept him in line. It was no real secret that Pastor's tight administrative rein even extended to a list of the principal contributors. Besides Pastor, only the treasurer and board chairman were supposed to know of "the list," but its existence was generally rumored throughout the church. It was also common knowledge that Pastor took those on the list out to an elegant lunch at the country club once a year.

In Stanley's first four years at Westside Church, he'd never had lunch with Pastor. Janet and Stan decided that giving ten dollars a week and fifty at Christmas and Easter was more than enough. For Stan, it was a point of pride *not* to do lunch with Pastor Whitehearst. He could be rather cold to those who didn't live up to his expectations—not exactly mean or unfriendly; it's just that whenever Stanley talked to him, Pastor used those twelve-dollar words with four-plus syllables like "countenancing" and "justification," and sometimes Stan had to get the dictionary.

Still, whether or not Stanley personally liked Pastor Whitehearst wasn't important. What mattered was that most everyone respected him. It couldn't be easy to govern a church, managing and maneuvering people from all walks of life. Moreover, Stanley knew that Pastor was truly loved by most of the members who had been there during the lean years. That included Janet and her family. After all, he had saved their church, and they were grateful. In fact, he had been so successful that the board talked about a major expansion project ahead.

The sermon ended right on time, and Stan gathered a few papers and prepared to leave. He waited in the foyer after Sunday school as Janet hung up her choir robe. Across the way, he caught sight of his employer, Barrett Kellene, who sat on the church board. To his surprise, Kellene made straight for him and took him aside. His seriousness alarmed Stan.

"Stanley, there's just no easy way to say this," Barrett said, clearing his throat expansively. "As you know, I'm the chairman of the official board and, of course, have knowledge of everyone's giving." Kellene dropped his voice and leaned his head a little closer. "If you were a little more generous, it would be a blessing to the church—and I know that some very interesting things would happen to you at work. It would be very pleasing to me if all the men who work for me were more involved in their churches. I believe it builds character in the individual, and that's good for the company and for the community."

As soon as they were back home and the girls were out of earshot, Stan told Janet about the conversation. They decided that they had better take the boss's advice.

'What do you think, honey?" Stan asked. "Twenty, no, we'd better go twenty-five a week, and a hundred at Christmas and Easter. Yes, I think that's about right. Let's try it for a while and see what happens." He snapped his wallet closed and shoved it in his pocket. "I'm so mad and embarrassed that I'd like to start looking for another job."

Janet seemed less upset. "Let's wait for a few months, Stan, and then we'll talk about another job, okay?"

Several months passed. Stanley's giving stayed consistent and he got the big promotion at work. Not only that, to his surprise, he was also invited to serve on the official board at church. With the raise, Janet and Stan were able to buy a beautiful home on the west side of town. They had finally made it, and they never again talked of new jobs.

Stan served on the board for about six months when the members assigned Stan to take over the job of the Treasurer, who had been ill. The day Stan discovered "the list" in his files, he realized that the rumors were indeed true. Twenty-five names filled the page and five of the first six were underlined. Everyone on the list would be treated to a nice lunch at the country club; the five underlined names would also be invited to the pastor's home for an elegant dinner.

Stanley frowned at the one exception: the third name on the list, the only one of the first six that wasn't underlined, Frank Jacobson, was never taken out to lunch or invited over to Pastor's home for dinner. And he had never served on the official board, unlike most of the names on the list. Stanley wracked his brains for what he knew about Frank. A big, warmhearted ex-alley fighter, Frank Jacobson was one of those "born again" Christians who was always stirring up trouble and trying to share his faith—with the best of intentions, of course.

Stanley's thoughts retreated to his first lunch with Pastor Whitehearst, a few months after adjusting his giving. He now knew, firsthand, what the ritual was.

After all the small talk about his job and family, Pastor would get to the nitty-gritty.

"Well, Stanley," he would say, "is there anything that Westside Church or I can do for you or your family?"

Stanley wanted to say "Make the service shorter" or some other smart remark, but he held his tongue.

"No, I can't think of anything at the moment. Everything is just fine. Thank you for asking." Of course, *everyone* said, "No, Pastor, everything is fine." Why should Stan do any different? Then Pastor Whitehearst would ask how Stan's church position as a member of the official board was going and if there was anything he could do to help. Of course, Stanley said no again.

"Well then, let me tell you what I'm trying to accomplish at the church, Stan."

"Oh, I'd love to hear about ..." Stan looked up to see an old friend darting toward him.

"Hi Stan. I don't mean to interrupt, I caught a glimpse of you from my table and just had to say hi. It's been so long."

"Oh, no worries, Dave. Let me introduce you to Pastor Whitehearst—a great man he is."

"Hello Mr. Whitehearst. Nice to meet you. Well, I don't want to interrupt at all. Okay.

Have a nice lunch y'all."

"Thanks Dave. I'll catch up with you soon."

"No problem." Dave waved walking back to his table.

"I'm sorry Pastor. You were saying..."

"Stanley," Pastor Whitehearst said sternly, "it would be more appropriate if you would introduce me as *Doctor* Whitehearst, Pastor of Westside Community Church. To our church family, I enjoy being called *Pastor,* but when encountering new people, I believe they should be made cognizant of my higher scholarship and the achievements that qualify me to lead Pinedale's finest church. After all, everyone in Pinedale is a prospective church member."

That self-righteous S.O.B., Stanley thought. He couldn't wait to tell Janet what Pastor said, although she would probably support him.

"Sorry, Pastor. Mr. Kellene told me how to introduce you. I just forgot. It won't happen again."

Even with that embarrassment, over time, Stanley's opinion of Pastor changed for the better. He now seemed so pleasant and kind that Stan began to see him in a new light and appreciate the task that he had undertaken at Westside Church.

Stanley placed "the list" back in its file cabinet, shaking his head with amusement at his memories—and at how his own heart had changed. *Giving twenty-five dollars a week is the best investment I ever made.* He often though. Somewhere along the line, Stanley became a real believer in what the Pastor preached: church attendance, plus getting involved in church affairs, produced a better and more rounded individual. And that was how people merited a heavenly eternity, along with baptism—and confirmation, of course.

The office door opened, and Stanley jumped. Turning to see Pastor Whitehearst, Stan was glad to know that the list was back in its sacred spot.

"Hi there, Stanley," Pastor Whitehearst said. "Sorry to disturb you. I think I left some sermon notes in here. Have you seen them?"

"Would these be them?" Stan asked, spotting a few misplaced papers on the desk.

"Yes, in fact," Pastor said. "Thank you."

"You're welcome," Stan said. In a sudden burst of warmth and pride in his new position, Stan continued, "And anything I can do for you, Pastor, you just ask me. I'm willing to help you, whenever and wherever I'm needed."

Later that evening, after the girls had gone to bed, Stan told Janet what he had said to Pastor Whitehearst. He'd kicked himself for it all the way home.

"You told Pastor what? That you would help him wherever and whenever, with church affairs?" Janet got up from her living-room chair, walked across the room, behind Stanley's chair, and put her hand on his forehead.

"I now pronounce you, Stanley M. Geraldson, brain-dead for sure."

"I know I'll be sorry. He'll probably be calling me all the time, asking me to do this or that. He just caught me at a weak moment, I guess."

Janet moved around from behind the chair and slid into Stan's lap.

"It is funny, but seriously, honey . . . Stan, I'm really very proud of you. You have really grown in the nine years we've been married. When I agreed to marry you, I did love you, but not as much as you loved me. I was looking more for security than for love. What I'm trying to say is that I love you very, very much—much more than I ever thought I would." She nestled closer. "I'm so glad that you have become more religious. It has made us a better, a stronger family—don't you think, Stan?"

"I do, honey." Stan reflected over the day and the last few years. They were certainly a much healthier and more loving family since becoming more active in church—happier and more contended than most, in fact. He told her as much. "And I do love you very much, sweetheart. In fact, it must be illegal to be this happy. I almost have to pinch myself every day to see if this is all real."

She laughed. "Now you're just being a smart aleck."

"Maybe," Stan grinned. "But a happy one."

8

OH NO, NOT THAT!

That same night, John Nelson opened his Bible. With its archaic wording and strange stories about angels, battles, and plagues, the Old Testament both drew him in and scared him. It surely didn't sound like the stuff he heard Pastor Whitehearst preach about. He looked at the clock—1:00.

The ruckus from the bars only grew louder. John knew it would be a while before the drunks passed out. The noise mirrored the turmoil in his own heart. He had been living over the gift shop for more than a year now, and his involvement in church had made him happier and more content—but sometimes, at night, he still thought back to his prayer for help and realized he needed something deeper. When it grew dark outside and he was alone, he still felt like the failure he knew he was. And no amount of church involvement was helping get over that.

John remembered reading about a military leader named Joshua, who came across a powerful armed warrior just before going into battle. He drew his sword and demanded to know whether the warrior was for him or for his enemies.

37

"Nay," the man—or maybe angel—said, "but as captain of the host of the LORD am I now come."

John shivered. Suddenly the story disturbed him. It seemed too much like God wanted *him* to make a decision to be on God's side but in a way his church didn't talk about. And somehow he knew that if he did, it would change his life. He just wasn't sure what this story was really trying to say. He went back to the story and continued reading. Near the end of the book of Joshua, John got a clear description of what the military leader was asking his people to do:

Throw away the gods your forefathers worshiped beyond the River and in Egypt, and serve the Lord. But if serving the Lord seems undesirable to you, then choose for yourselves this day whom you will serve, whether the gods your forefathers served beyond the River, or the gods of the Amorites, in whose land you are living. But as for me and my household, we will serve the Lord.

John fixated on that last sentence, *But as for me and my household, we will serve the Lord.* Restless, John put the Bible aside and flicked on the TV. For some reason, it was on a preaching channel.

"... and Jesus said, you must be born again!" the preacher proclaimed. John heard this before, on a street corner somewhere or maybe on some other station. He wanted to change the station, but yet he didn't.

"Your good deeds can't make you good enough for God. Your religion doesn't win you brownie points with God. Your church position and nice family don't make you right with Him. Folks, hell is a real place, and unless you are born again by faith in Jesus Christ, that's where you're going!"

John walked over to the TV, intending to turn the obnoxious preacher off. But just before he did, the preacher seemed to look him straight in the eye. "Not only that," the preacher said, "but Jesus is coming back. Maybe today. Maybe tomorrow. And He's going to ask whose side you are on. What are you going to answer?"

The next evening, after putting the girls to bed, Janet and Stanley sat on the couch with their favorite cocktail. *Mary Tyler Moore* just started, Janet's favorite. Stan reached around Janet as the doorbell rang. Swinging his arm back, Stan reached over to turn down the TV as Janet headed for the door.

"John, how nice to see you. Is everything okay? Come in, come in." Janet ushered John into the living room. Flushed with excitement, John barely waited to be seated on the couch before he launched into his reason for coming.

"I've found out the truth about Jesus."

"What are you talking about?" Janet asked softly. "We all know the truth about Jesus."

John shook his head. "No, no, you don't—not really. They don't preach it at the church. Listen, there is a heaven and hell, and I've come to tell you what you must do to be saved. You two are closer than anyone else in the world to me, and you know how much I love your girls. It's just that Jesus is coming soon to judge this wicked and sinful world. You must confess that you are sinners and repent, or you are going to hell."

Stanley and Janet looked at each other in disbelief.

"John, you *know* that we're good Christian people. We thank you for your concern, but maybe we'd better talk about this when you're a little less excited."

"I'm not crazy," John said. "I was reading my Bible last night, and there was this preacher on TV who talked about our need to be born again. Well, I did what he said. I prayed and repented and told God I wanted a new life. And then I flicked the TV back on and watched that preacher and several others most of the night—I learned so much. He talked all about the end times and spiritual warfare and how everyone is headed for damnation if they don't get right with God."

"John, I think that you better ..."

"No. See, you two just don't know that Satan is the god of this world and that Jesus is the only way to heaven. He wants us to repent of our sin so we won't go to Hell. Will you do that with me?"

"We've heard enough." Stanley firmly grasped John's arm and escorted him to the door.

Stanley stood on the front porch, shaking with anger. *How dare he come and accost us like this!*

"You are not to set foot in . . . I don't think you should come to our house again if you are going to act like this. John, I think you need help. You're acting very strange."

As John walked dejectedly toward his car, Stan shouted out, "John, we are very happy with our beliefs! If you want to change your religion, that's fine, but don't try to force your holier-than-thou beliefs on us. And don't you ever call us sinners." The anger inside Stanley welled up even higher. "We're not sinners; we're a good Christian family, and we are trying very hard to do the best we can."

As they sat on the couch together, Janet cuddled up close. "Stan, I'm frightened. I can't stop shaking . . . what should we do? What right does he have to say that we're going to hell?"

"I don't know what to say, honey. Maybe the stress from his financial problems and the humiliation of having to move back to the east side has caused some kind of breakdown." Stan was quiet. "All I know is, he's wrong. We've worked hard to get where we are. If John can't be content to make a living and earn success like everybody else, well . . . that's his problem, not ours."

John drove home angry and embarrassed and upset, but mostly distressed for his friends. *Why couldn't they see that going to church isn't enough to make them right with God? Satan really must have blinded them!* John concluded.

When he reached his apartment, John flicked on his TV. A stack of books and magazines about the end times and prophecy stood precariously next to it—he had picked them all up at a local bookshop that morning. The preacher was back on TV, raving about hell and the end of the world.

Maybe I just need to be more passionate, John thought as he watched the preacher. *I have to convince people like Stanley of the truth. They've just got to listen!*

As soon as the commercials came on, John began to read one of the books. *Yes, I need to be stronger and more passionate in how I witness, even if it's hard. I just have to get people to listen—any way I can.*

In the weeks that followed, John became the talk of the town, mostly they talked about how he had turned into a real religious nut. He was telling everyone who would listen—and even those who didn't want to—that they were going to hell if they didn't repent of their sins.

John said this in the nightclubs, taverns, pool hall, and other businesses along Worth Street. It got so commonplace that when John walked down one side of the street, everyone—except the tourists who didn't know any better—would cross to the other side or go into one of the shops in hopes that he would pass them by.

Stanley, Janet, and many of the townsfolk wondered how John, being so shy, could now be so bold in his so-called "witnessing for Jesus." No one changed their beliefs; rather, John frightened some of the people with his decrees of "Repent, for the kingdom of God is near!" Hearing about judgment, damnation, and despair was not popular in Pinedale.

Friends and acquaintances would ask Stanley about John, since they knew he had been John's best friend. The only thing Stan could think to tell them was that John had cracked under the humiliation of his business failure.

Soon, John became the butt of many jokes. Even those in Stanley's realm of friends and coworkers wondered aloud how long it would take before he would start carrying a sign with big bold letters: "YOU'RE GOING TO HELL" on one side and "JESUS LOVES YOU" on the other. Stanley had to admit—to his shame—that he told as many jokes about John as they did.

"Repent, before it's too late and Hell is all you'll ever see!" cried John in the lot behind his building.

"You're crazy man," slurred a drunkard.

"Yeah, dude. You're the one going to hell for what you're doing," shouted a bystander.

"The two of you are going to hell if you don't repent of your sins and turn to Jesus. Why won't you listen to the gospel?" John pleaded.

The drunk replied, "We're not listening to your garbage, preacher man. Going to hell is fine with us; after all, that's where all our friends are going, too."

Crowds were quickly leaving the back doors of the bars to gather in the parking lot.

"You may not know it, preacher man, but you're in a no-no-no-preaching zone, and we're going to make a citizen's arrest."

Before John could protest, he threw a punch straight at his face. Large rings on the men's fingers made their punches doubly damaging. Even so, John didn't fight back. When the beating got rather vicious, several in the crowd tried to make them stop. A young woman from the jewelry store down the street turned to her husband with tear-filled eyes.

"Bruce, please help him! Make them stop; he wasn't hurting anyone!"

Bruce Wills folded his arms. "He's getting just what he deserved, Vicky, preaching all the time. He drives the tourists away with his 'gospel of Jesus.' He's just another self-righteous loser."

Bruce cried out with others, "Hit him again, hit him again!" Vicky rushed back into the bar to call the police.

John finally lost consciousness as the wail of police sirens could be heard in the distance. The thugs gave him one last kick in the ribs, tossed him into a nearby dumpster, and ran into the darkness of the night.

When the police arrived, John had just regained consciousness, although his words slurred and didn't make much sense. The police had seen John preaching on the streets before, but with so much blood and lacerations on his face, they couldn't recognize him. They helped him out of the dumpster and tried to stop the bleeding as best they could. At the hospital, x-rays showed two cracked ribs and a broken jaw. Eighty-eight stitches closed the cuts on his face. The police tried to get a description of the men, but John wouldn't give any.

After Stanley heard about the attack, he stopped telling "John jokes." It wasn't funny anymore; and anyway, John was no longer on the streets with his hell-and-damnation preaching. He realized that his witnessing had failed. In effect, all he had accomplished was achieving the title of "town fool."

For more than a month, John didn't attend church or work in his shop. He had let God down with his lack of success in presenting the gospel to lost souls. Locked in his apartment, he decided that he would read the Bible from cover to cover instead of just those portions on end-time prophecy. In fact, in all his prayers, he began to ask God for wisdom and soon discovered in the Bible several people who, like him, had great zeal for the Lord but lacked wisdom.

John didn't know when God would answer his prayer, but he hoped that he wouldn't be kept waiting too long, for he had little patience. *Even if God were to answer my prayers, who would ever listen to me again?* The answer, he felt, was to move out of town. He was certain his credibility in Pinedale could never be restored. John quietly hired an out-of-town business broker to try to sell his building and his business.

That night, John walked down the streets of east-side Pinedale. It was too cold for many people to be out in the streets, so the night was unusually quiet. He could hear the river in the distance and see the neon lights coloring the sky, as always.

As he walked, he became aware of footsteps near him.

He looked behind him. A few steps back, a big man with long, golden hair, his hands stuffed in a winter coat, kept pace with him.

"Cold, isn't it?" the man asked, catching up to John.

"Yeah," John replied.

"Not just the night. Your heart too."

"I guess so," John said. He shook his head. "I've ruined a whole lot of things by trying to be zealous or 'hot' for God. I love Him so much, but nobody respects anything I have to say. I'm pretty sure the best thing I can do for Him now is get out of town."

The stranger shook his head. "You know, the Lord isn't angry with you for messing up. Yes, you need to learn wisdom—and God has heard your prayers for wisdom, and He will give it to you. But He's always glad to see someone really wanting to serve Him and witness for Him."

Rather than being afraid at his words, John felt strangely peaceful and safe.

"But I've only turned people away!" John burst out.

"Maybe," the man said. "But God can still work in their hearts. The message you gave is still with them, and several are wondering where they will spend their eternity. You need to go back to church, John."

"That church?" John snorted. "I don't believe anyone there is even saved."

The stranger's eyes twinkled. "I think you'll be surprised if you go back. The Lord has a few things planned for you."

"Really?" John asked.

"Really," the stranger told him.

John stopped walking. "Who are you, anyway?"

The stranger smiled. "My name is Gedaliah. It means 'Yahweh is great.'"

"What's your last name?" John inquired further.

"It's just Gedaliah," the stranger answered. "You just stay on the Lord's side, John Nelson. You'll see Him do great things yet."

"It's bad enough to go to church on Sundays, but on Saturday too? There should be a law against it," Stanley said as he started the car for the short drive to Westside Church.

"I know you'll be bored to death, Stan, but it's only one Saturday a year, and you'll probably live through it," Janet chided. "It's not too much to ask. We've chosen to be a good church family, and I guess we can give up one Saturday a year for our church. Look at our Catholic friends! Some of them go to Mass several times a week."

"Okay, okay. You know that I just like to complain." Stanley stayed silent as they drove down the manicured streets of the west side. Abruptly, he said, "Not to change the subject, honey, but I've had a dream two or three times in the last month, and I've been wanting to tell you about it. Your mention of being a good church family reminded me. Now is as good a time as any."

"Well?" Janet said. "Go on."

Stanley pulled up to a red light. "In the dream, I'm walking through the streets of Pinedale at night turning off the lights. I don't want to turn off the lights, but I just can't stop. They're so beautiful when they're on, but I keep turning them off. Do you think I should be concerned about it? Do you think my conscience is trying to tell me something? Is it about John and his strange actions?"

Janet hesitated. "Stan, it's just a dream. All dreams are weird, and nobody really knows what they mean. I wouldn't worry about it if I were you."

Stanley wasn't convinced, but he left it at that. They drove the rest of the way to Westside Church and found their usual parking spot.

It was Pastor Whitehearst's annual retreat held every year in the church parlor. The room was about twenty feet wide and more than twice as long. A large, exquisite picture window looked out over the manicured lawn and newly surfaced parking lot at the back of the church. Smaller stained-glass windows bordered either side of the large window.

Five elegant choice sofas, several love seats, and comfy chairs strategically furnished the room. Artistic cabinets lined the walls with beautiful, tasteful paintings above them—brilliant fields of flora and fauna, and reproductions of famous portraits—but none of Christ or any other religious figures. Except for the stained-glass windows, nothing indicated that the room belonged to a church.

The Geraldsons walked toward the window, stopping every few feet to say hi to church friends and even a polite hello as they walked by John. He was sitting alone, an empty chair on either side of him. Stan and Janet found two comfortable chairs, one on each side of a small corner table across the room.

Janet whispered, "I never expected John to be here, did you, Stan? Those scars on his face, I didn't think they would be so noticeable. They're awful!"

John's face had mostly healed from the beating. But one rather large scar started at the corner of his mouth on the right side of his face and extended almost to his ear. In the opinion of many, including Stan and Janet, this scar would always be a mark and a reminder of his misguided actions and tarnished reputation.

"I'm surprised, too, Hon." Stan said. "I wonder if he's going to get plastic surgery—he could sure use it." Stanley didn't say what else he was thinking. In the past, this meeting had always been by invitation only—to those on "the list." He only muttered to himself, "I just hope John keeps his mouth shut today."

Pastor Whitehearst opened the meeting with a prayer from his prayer book. Other church leaders read their prayers, poems, short stories and speeches. After an hour and a half, all but a few found the entire time thoroughly boring.

Still sitting alone, John listened with increasing agitation. *What does any of this have to do with Jesus?* John thought. *Why did I talk myself into coming anyway? Then again, Gedaliah did tell me I needed to get back to church, and I need to start getting into the mainstream of life again. Sitting at home by myself has to stop. They're all wondering if I'm going to start preaching again. Am I the only one saved at this church? Lord, what do you want me to do? I'm ready to do whatever you want.*

As the last prepared reading ended, Pastor stood.

"I would like to use the next hour or so for some of you to relate some of the ways attendance at Westside Church and your faith in God has made your lives more meaningful."

Barrett Kellene began by saying how being involved at Westside Church had helped to bring fulfillment and completeness to his family's lives.

Then it was Stanley's turn. *Help,* he thought. He stood up and cleared his throat.

"Well, I must say . . . yes . . . I agree with Barrett's statements." Then the words started to come: "It's . . . it's hard to put into words, but I think that somehow our lives would not be complete, wouldn't be as rich, without our responsibilities and associations here at Westside Church. I mean . . . when I first got involved here, it was work, work that I really didn't want to do. Now that I understand what our pastor is trying to accomplish here, I've truly come to enjoy my commitment here at Westside. I really believe it helps me to be a better husband and father."

Stanley could see that Pastor Whitehearst was very pleased with his statement of faith. Stan was pretty pleased himself. Back in his seat, Janet made a hushed sucking sound that only Stanley heard. "What was it you said as we left the house this morning, Stan?"

"Shush," Stan answered.

Next, to everyone's surprise, Jane Kime said that she asked Christ into her heart at the age of fourteen and her life had been changed ever since. Next, Frank Jacobson gave his testimony of becoming a born-again Christian. The big man spoke with passion, conviction, and less-than-educated language.

A few in the room were growing teary-eyed, clearly moved by his words. The majority by contrast, were squirming in their chairs. Four more women gave similar testimonies making Pastor Whitehearst think he lost control of the meeting. He never imagined it turning into a Westside Jesus revival. Stanley was almost getting sick to his stomach and wondered why this talk of Jesus made people so uncomfortable. He also wondered why he hadn't stayed home and cleaned the garage.

To his dismay, Stanley caught sight of John scribbling something down on a napkin—names? Was he recording the names of those who, like him, were born-again Christians?

As soon as the last woman stopped speaking, John jumped to his feet with a new surge of confidence and started to give his testimony.

"I would like to tell you all about my—"

Stanley smiled as big as ever when Pastor Whitehearst put his hand on John's arm, stopping him in mid-sentence.

"About time," Stan said, not softly enough, and several nearby heard. Janet glared at Stan and not-so-gently kicked him in the ankle while giving him one of those looks. Stanley called it the "disparaging evil eye."

"It is admirable that some of you have attestations of this nature," Pastor Whitehearst said. "I have always voiced the conviction that there is room for everyone who believes in God, whether you're here by virtue of our softball team or your profound faith. As long as no one endeavors to thrust his or her faith or doctrine on another member, there is room here for all who strive to follow God through baptism, confirmation, church membership, and living life as the most exceptional personage one can be."

Pastor Whitehearst thanked everyone for their participation, then closed the retreat with a prayer from his prayer book and issued an invitation for everyone to have coffee and rolls in the fellowship hall.

9

BIG JAKE

John didn't feel like eating donuts. He stayed behind, sitting at a corner table with his head in his hands.

"John, may I join you?"

John raised his eyes to see a smiling Frank Jacobson. Quietly he answered, "Okay."

Most people referred to Frank as Big Jake, although never to his face. Big Jake was in his early forties, over six-foot-three, and weighed well over two hundred pounds. He had huge hands and a muscular frame. What hair he had left, he combed over the bald spot on top of his head.

As usual, Big Jake wore a suit and tie. Except for Pastor Whitehearst, everyone else had dressed casually. But the suit wasn't off-putting. Frank was always ready to help anyone in need. He carried a small New Testament in his shirt pocket so he would be ready to witness about his faith in Jesus whenever the opportunity arose. He sang in the choir, held the title of a deacon and a Christian from the wrong side of Worth Street. He was quietly kept off the official board; and even though he taught about Jesus in Sunday school, he was only allowed to teach the younger kids, never anyone older than twelve.

Still, even the pastor had to admit that Frank was useful for some things. Pastor Whitehearst was quite uncomfortable with visiting the very sick and dying, and he would often ask Frank to make those calls for him. When people were hurting, Big Jake was always there with loving words and a long prayer. When Big Jake prayed, it was as if he were talking directly to God. He never needed to use a prayer book; he would just start praying.

The church put up with Big Jake because he never tried to force his beliefs on anyone as John had done. Most everyone respected Frank because they felt he really loved them—although they didn't want to get too close and chummy, or he would take his little New Testament out of his shirt pocket and attempt to lead them to Jesus.

"I enjoyed your testimony a few minutes ago," John said. "For some reason, I thought I was the only real Christian at Westside. After hearing the others telling how they came to know Christ, well, now I know that there are at least seven of us here."

Frank smiled. "John, I know of at least fifteen Christians at our church. Now, out of three hundred and fifty members, that's nothing to be proud of. But if you remember the story of Elijah in the Old Testament, in 1 Kings I think, where he told God that he was the only one left and it turned out that there were seven thousand that belonged to God—well, there are probably others that we don't even know about." The big man chuckled. "Not everyone can have a past as interesting as yours and mine."

John smiled. He had heard about Frank's stormy youth, from which he had received his nickname. His reputation as an alley fighter was legendary. One of those fights involved a semi-professional boxer of some stature who delivered many timely blows to Big Jake's face. Finally, Big Jake just grabbed him by the collar with his left hand, and with a windmill-type delivery, hit the boxer on the top of his head with his closed fist.

The boxer woke up in the hospital a few hours later and wasn't released until the next day. The police investigated, but the boxer wouldn't say who injured him; or rather, he only said he couldn't remember. A few years later, Big Jake got saved, and that turbulent part of his life came to an end. Now his battles involved making an impact on a Christ-rejecting world.

Frank looked directly into John's eyes, and with deep concern said, "I'm sorry that Pastor Whitehearst didn't allow you to give your testimony, but would you tell me your story?"

John could see the love and compassion in Big Jake's eyes, and for the first time since he'd spilled his story to the mysterious stranger that he had encountered; he truly opened up. He told Frank about his business failure and even his loneliness. He told about his TV-evangelist watching and his reading of several books on Bible prophecy and realizing that he must be living in the last days. He told Big Jake the complete story about his encounter with the stranger and his thoughts that's this mysterious stranger might be and angel.

Big Jake took out his New Testament and went over several Scriptures with John, "This is just to make sure you covered all the bases in your conversion. It's not enough to just ask Christ into your life, John. You must also live your life pleasing to Christ."

"I do know that I'm a sinner. I really do. I have also assured God that I never want to go back to the cheating, lying, and lustful life I lived before. I have repented of that."

Frank chuckled and apologized for his concern. "Truth is, Frank. I thought you were involved with some kind of cult. I'm sorry I didn't make an effort to talk with you sooner."

As their conversation neared the end, John's face perked up, looking more focused and alive than in a long time. "Frank, why don't we born-again Christians at Westside Church start meeting every week for a prayer and praise time?"

Big Jake nodded slowly. There had been just such a group in the past, but it had broken up. As for John—well, he had a lot to learn, but he was certainly a Christian. He just had a lot of rough edges, that was all. A prayer and praise group with some Bible study was just what John needed.

"John, I think your idea is great. Not only that, but I believe now is a perfect time to get a group like this going in our church. I'll make some calls and try to set something up."

As Frank stood, he laid a meaty hand on John's shoulder. "Son, I believe that God brought you to Westside Church for some special reason. I'll call you tomorrow, hopefully with the time and place of the first meeting."

10

IT'S NOT TIME YET

The newly formed group met for the first time at Frank and Sandra Jacobson's home the following week. They called themselves the Westside Prayer and Praise Group, which they shortened to the WPAP. After a few months, John's apartment, affectionately called the Upper Room, became the meeting hub filled once a week with singing, prayer, and Bible study.

Even though the group was John's idea, Big Jake showed himself to be a natural leader, and that was just fine with John. John still blurted out from time to time his thoughts about Jesus's second coming, the antichrist, Satan being the god of this world, and the end of the world, but for the most part he listened to Frank and the others in the group and began to grow in his Christian walk. John's enthusiasm for Jesus influenced their lives as well.

The WPAP included Frank and Sandra Jacobson, Jane Kime, who played her guitar for the singing, Chelsea Bue,

Susan Howard, and Marion Nyberg, along with John. Others joined them from time to time.

The group made it their goal to show God's love to their town, and they did so in many practical ways. They prayed especially hard for revival at Westside Church, including the salvation of Pastor Whitehearst, whom they were all convinced was "lost" meaning "not saved." They prayed for the four unsaved husbands of the women in the group and, at John's request, for the Geraldson family. Within two years, all four of the husbands began to attend some of the meetings, and three of them eventually became born-again Christians. The Geraldsons, though, seemed untouchable. To John's deep grief, Stanley seemed almost hostile to him whenever they met.

At the next church board meeting, Pastor Whitehearst took Stanley and Barrett Kellene and two others aside to tell them of the WPAP. "This group is going to cause problems at Westside Church. I can feel it in my bones," the pastor told them.

"I've heard," Stan said, "that they're praying for us—they want us to become born-again Christians like themselves. Pastor, how can they believe that they know the only way to heaven?"

Pastor shook his head sadly. "Somehow these groups get so emotional and fanatical that they become intolerant of everyone else. Keep your eyes and ears open, and communicate to me the moment you hear anything. Groups like this can undermine and destroy a church. I want to know especially what John Nelson and Frank Jacobson are up to. I realize there's not much we can do at this time. We will just have to wait for an opportunity to deal with this group."

"Doctor Whitehearst," Barrett Kellene interjected, "my daughter is in John's Sunday school class, and even though she thinks he's wonderful, I personally don't like what he has been teaching. Is it possible that that after this quarter is over . . ."

"Yes, I see what you're getting at. I had planned to replace John next spring, at the end of the Sunday school year." Pastor Whitehearst looked more uncomfortable than Stanley had ever seen him. "It's just so unpleasant to remove someone—it creates so much gossip and bad feelings, and it might give the Westside Prayer and Praise Group a martyr. The last thing we want to do is make them angry. No, I think it best if we keep John right where he is. Since his beating, he hasn't caused any real problems. I'll keep a close watch on things."

Seeing that Barrett Kellene wasn't satisfied, Pastor continued, "I'll talk to the Sunday school superintendent and advise her to ask John to follow the curriculum precisely."

As Stanley drove home that night, he was concerned. How could they keep these born-again zealots from infecting the entire congregation? Why couldn't these Jesus freaks move to another church? After all, there were one or two holy-roller churches on the east side of town.

Nevertheless, everything seemed to be going fine for Westside Church. Two years passed. The Westside Prayer and Praise Group grew to over a dozen people, yet they didn't cause any problems for the church. Even John seemed to mellow over the months. He wasn't seen preaching on the streets any longer, and Stan and Janet even had polite conversations with him at church on Sunday mornings. Courtney and Stephanie still loved John; the adult politics and ill-feelings toward John had not rubbed off on them.

Many times after the WPAP Group meetings, Chelsea and Marion would invite John to join them for coffee and pie at a downtown restaurant for another half hour or so. They took a special interest in John, for they saw the deep sadness in his blue eyes. The three became close friends.

One week, as they sipped coffee, Chelsea laid her hand on John's, exchanged a troubled glance with Marion, and said, "John, we've been talking, and well, you really don't look well. You're so thin, and from time to time you look like you're in pain. Have you seen a doctor?"

Marion chimed in, "You should have some tests done."

Chelsea ignored John shaking his head. "Yes, John, the whole group is very concerned about you. Would you humor us and get a good checkup?"

"I'm fine," John said. "I've had an upset stomach from time to time—I just need to eat some better foods. Thanks for your concern, but I'm really okay." He laughed at the looks on their faces. "If it continues, I promise you I'll see a doctor."

As he walked home that night, no laughter entered John's thoughts as he considered the conversation. He assured them again that he was fine—but he knew how many dozens of pain pills and antacid tablets he had been taking every day for stomach and intestinal pain.

John wasn't sure why he was afraid to go to the doctor. It might have been a combination of things, the most prominent being his father's gruesome death. The cancer treatment his father went through, John thought, was in many ways more devastating than the cancer itself. He realized that the doctors were doing the best they could, but he believed they had just dragged out the inevitable. His grandfather had also died of cancer at an early age. Secretly, John had always believed that he, too, would never reach his fortieth birthday. Yet, now he was a Christian, and in the back of his mind he felt that if there was something seriously wrong, Jesus would heal him. He just knew that Big Jake was right about God having a special purpose for him, and he wouldn't die until that objective was fulfilled.

11

THE WRONG ANSWER

"My dad says there's no heaven or hell," yelled a boy in John's Sunday school class. Not only did John correct the young boy, he told the class, "Less than twenty people at Westside Church are saved and the rest are going to hell if they didn't repent of their sins and put all their faith in Jesus." This was a little heavy for fourth- and fifth-grade children, to say the least. Frightened, many told their parents what John taught them.

Pastor Whitehearst wasn't halfway through his Sunday lunch that day when the phone started ringing. The rest of the afternoon was spent trying to calm irate parents. They demanded that John be removed from teaching Sunday school, and a meeting was hastily called for the following evening at the church.

Many of the parents from John's Sunday school class attended, along with Miss Paulson, the Sunday school superintendent, and several members of the official board, including Stanley and Barrett Kellene. They all agreed that

John had to be removed from teaching Sunday school. Pastor Whitehearst asked Miss Paulson to confront John.

"I realize that it's my responsibility to acquire and replace teachers," said Miss Paulson, "but I feel that the seriousness of this situation calls for the pastor to take the action."

Several of the parents agreed with her. They all knew that Pastor Whitehearst did not like confrontations and avoided them whenever possible, but the group turned almost as one and waited for him to respond.

It didn't take long for Pastor Whitehearst to come up with a scheme to accomplish this uncomfortable task. "Since there are only three weeks left in the fall quarter, parents who want to may keep their children out of Sunday school until the next quarter starts, which is the first Sunday in December. If there are only two or three children in his class, that will certainly send a message to John. At that time, Miss Paulson will inform John that because of the low attendance and with my approval, we are forced to get someone else to teach his class the rest of the church year."

Pastor Whitehearst asked Stanley and Barrett Kellene to stay after the meeting. As the last of the parents and board members left the boardroom, he turned to them and said, "First, I feel that I owe Barrett an apology, for you advised me to remove John from teaching two years ago. I should have taken your advice. I am sorry, Barrett."

"Thank you, Pastor, but there is no need for an apology. At the time it was a good decision."

Pastor Whitehearst nodded, his face showing that he wasn't happy. "I trust you realize this decision may be only a short-term solution. Eventually, as pastor, I may have to ask John to leave Westside Church. This is the most forbidding responsibility a pastor has. As you know, I am not comfortable with this sort of situation. Whereas it is Miss Paulson's job as Sunday school superintendent to confront John in her department, it will be my responsibility to entreat John to vacate the church."

Pastor straightened his shoulders and continued. "When John first joined the church, he had my approbation. I admired him very much. But now he is tearing my congregation apart, and I will not stand for it. Since the Christmas season is nearly upon us, I'll wait until after the first of the year to confront John. As you well know, approximately one third of the year's pledges are paid in the last six weeks of the year. I don't want any controversy, variances, or animosity at this most critical period. I have a lot planned for 1977.

"But there is at least one more uncertainty: the WPAP Group. What will they do if John is asked to leave the church? They're all top contributors, and if they leave, the church will have financial problems for a long time to come. Our plans for remodeling the church would have to be delayed or canceled. I disagree with their extreme Christianity, yet they are all highly regarded throughout the church. Except for John, of course."

Stanley interrupted. "Pastor, I feel responsible for this mess. As you know, I'm the one who invited John to visit this church in the first place, although John and I hardly talk anymore since he became one of those Jesus freaks. If you want, although I would rather not, I'll talk to him about this problem."

"That won't be necessary, Stanley. This is one of the most distasteful things a pastor has to do, but it is one responsibility I cannot pass off. I would appreciate it if you would accompany me when the time comes, however."

"Yes," Stanley said as he reluctantly nodded his head in agreement.

"Just maybe something will transpire in the next six weeks, and we will not have to take this drastic action," added Pastor Whitehearst. "Since there isn't a specific prayer in my prayer book that fits this impasse, I have written out a prayer that I believe covers the situation. I'm not sure that God has any concern for our difficulties here at Westside Church, but I do know that we cannot afford to leave Him out of any possible solution. Gentlemen, would you bow your heads please?"

As Barrett and Stanley bowed their heads, Pastor Whitehearst began.

"Dear and glorious God, we humbly come before You with heavy hearts. We ask for Your deliverance from this time of trial at Westside Church. We ask that You, dear God, would dispense Your divine justice over John Nelson and the group that he and Frank Jacobson have formed. Oh, God, hear our prayer. Lead us out of this time of tribulation and deliver us from these individuals who would divide and destroy this church. Amen."

With that, Pastor Whitehearst thanked Stanley and Barrett for their attendance, and all went home.

12

DISRUPTION IN TOWN

V icky Wills crossed Worth Street headed for her job at an exclusive gift shop. On this third Saturday in November, most of the stores had already been open about an hour.

Crossing the street, she headed into John's small gift-and-card shop where she put some things away for Christmas. Ever since the day she'd witnessed John's beating, he'd been on her mind. Oh, she knew all the crazy stories about him, but what had happened to him wasn't right. She had even tried to give the police a description of the two men who assaulted him, but her husband, Bruce, wouldn't allow it. He physically dragged her away from them.

She didn't see much of John for a long time after the beating. The last few months he was spending more time in his shop than before—she thought business must be slow. Before the beating, he had two full-time and two or three part-time employees. Vicky knew this because John asked if she would work for him. He had offered her more money than she now made, but Bruce said no; and furthermore, he didn't even want her to shop in his store.

A cold, snowy breeze blew past as Vicky opened the door and stepped inside, a small bell jingling to announce her entrance. What Bruce didn't know wouldn't hurt him. John didn't seem overly religious to her, although he said, "May the Lord bless your day" every time she left his store. And like everyone else, she wondered about those sad blue eyes. Was he as lonely and unhappy as he looked?

John was helping a customer select a gift, and a young part-timer was stocking the shelves nearby. "Good morning, Vicky," John said. "I'll be with you in a minute."

"That's okay, John," Vicky said, taking quiet note of his thin frame and gaunt face, with his cheekbones quite visible. *He doesn't look well,* she thought. "I'll just browse for a while."

Reaching for a box on the top shelf, John bent over and cried out in excruciating pain. He collapsed to the floor. Vicky rushed to his side, then shouted to the stock boy, "Call an ambulance!" She and the customer bent down to see if they could be of any aid. John lay on his side, clutching his stomach and moaning softly. His blue eyes were glazed with pain. A few moments later, he cried out again, and then his body went limp."

"Is he dead?" asked the stock boy, moving closer. "No, I don't think so," said Vicky. "I think he just passed out. I hear the ambulance. Go hold the door for them."

Still unconscious, the paramedics wasted no time getting him to the hospital. Vicky helped the stock boy close the store and went to work very concerned. An hour or so later, a helicopter flew John to a Minneapolis hospital.

John's stepfather called Big Jake Saturday night, "John has intestinal cancer," he said. "The doctors operated on him for several hours. They cleaned out as many tumors as they could, but the cancer has spread into too many organs. They can't stop it. This is difficult to believe and say, but they only gave him one or maybe two more months to live."

As the news of John's cancer spread throughout the church Sunday morning, everyone who knew him seemed to forget about the disruptions he had caused. Several of the women of the WPAP were crying while their husbands tried to console them.

When the Geraldsons arrived at church, they were surprised by the commotion but even more surprised to overhear Frank talking about the surgery. "What happened?" Stephanie asked. Janet's voice was steady but grieved as she explained that John was very sick and was in a hospital in Minneapolis.

Courtney looked up at her dad with her big brown eyes and asked, "Is Uncle John going to die, Daddy?"

Stanley bent down and took her into his arms. She knew the answer. "Oh, no! No, Daddy, no!" She and Stephanie sobbed uncontrollably. Stanley watched them with his jaw tight and grim. Even though John was no longer a frequent guest at their home, the girls still loved their Uncle John.

Frank Jacobson gathered the Prayer and Praise Group around him in the corner of the foyer, and they knelt down as Big Jake lead them in prayer.

Pastor Whitehearst just stood by the sanctuary doors with his mouth open, amazed at what he was seeing and not understanding any of it. Behind him, light shone brightly through the stained-glass window, with its powerful winged angel seemingly concerned. Some of his congregation kneeling in the foyer and praying—he had never seen such an exhibition of prayer before. Happy to be near service time, he encouraged everyone to take their seats in the sanctuary and the choir to form up at the main doors to the sanctuary. When he stepped inside, the organist took her cue and started playing the prelude.

Stan and Janet decided to skip the church service and take the girls home.

"Stan, take the girls to the car while I explain to the choir leader that I won't be singing, okay? I'll meet you at the car in a couple of minutes."

Janet sat in the back of the car with the girls as Stan drove. She tried to ease their pain, but she broke down, too. When they got home, Stanley tried to comfort the three of them. He sat on the living room couch with his arm around his wife and their daughters on their laps, but as much as he tried to suppress their tears, his own finally began to flow. Now Janet and the girls tried to console Stanley.

Back at church, Pastor Whitehearst's spoke on how to have a cheerful and meaningful life. After ten minutes, though, he admitted, "In light of the circumstances of this weekend, I believe this topic may not be the most appropriate. Before I close, allow me to read a prayer for John Nelson from my prayer book."

Over the next weeks, Stanley contemplated the consequences of the prayer that Pastor Whitehearst had written to ask God to intervene and save Westside Church from John and the WPAP Group. He couldn't believe that God would answer Pastor's prayer in this manner. Could it be that one man would die for the good of the congregation? It would certainly solve most of the problems at Westside Church. Feelings of sorrow and guilt immersed Stan. Deep inside, he knew that John had a profound love for the people of Westside Church, a love much stronger than his own. Even all that business about people going to hell was inspired by love—a love that dared to speak up.

The next Sunday, Pastor asked several board members to stay after church for a short meeting.

"I just need to tell you all that I am not delighted with the way circumstances have evolved," he said once they were comfortably seated in the boardroom. "I am not gratified by John's illness. Please do not communicate to the members of this congregation any idea that his illness could be the consequence of my prayer. This is just a coincidence. On the contrary, I am deeply concerned for John, and I have been praying for him. I hope you are also doing so."

As several of them nodded, Pastor Whitehearst went on. "I've asked myself, 'Why has this one man so disrupted our church?' In the last two weeks, a dozen or more members have asked me if the things John was asserting regarding salvation are true. I assured them that they are not. Yes, at times I have doubts—don't we all? But I will adhere to what I have been taught since my youth, which was confirmed by my seminary training. God's all-encompassing grace is perspicuous and covers any who are baptized and confirmed and who make an effort to lead a righteous life. If we cling to what we know is true, peace will be restored here once again."

"Bruce? Are you home? Honey?" Vicki Wills shouted as she entered the apartment. Only silence answered. A terrible fear struck her. He had been acting so angry and strange lately, like he didn't care about their home or their marriage or anything else, except himself.

Vicky went to the kitchenette. Biting her lip, she picked up a note on the table. Reading it quickly, she fought to keep back the tears as her eyes fixated on the last line, "I won't be coming back." It was true. Bruce was gone.

Vicky collapsed on the threadbare couch giving herself permission to cry and cry a lot. What was she going to do? What were the boys going to do? She forced herself to get up again. A few more minutes of investigation made it clear: Bruce had cleaned out their joint account and removed all of his things and some of hers. Rent and utilities were due in a few days.

For some reason, Vicky thought of John at the store. If only he hadn't gotten sick! She could have taken the job he'd offered her and begged him to pay her before her first pay period. He was such a kind man, with a genuine concern for people, even if he was kind of crazy. He would have helped her.

Maybe John's God can help, Vicky thought suddenly. As her feelings of hopelessness grew, she bowed her head and prayed for help for her and her sons.

In the few weeks before Christmas, the Westside Prayer and Praise Group continued with their weekly meetings. Much of their time was spent in prayer for John. In the beginning, they thought God would surely heal John, but as the weeks went by and his condition only worsened, all but Big Jake began to lose hope. Even with the absence of John, the WPAP Group meetings had grown to more than twenty. It seemed that many people of the church were wondering about the things that John used to say so loudly, wondering if they were true. Still, few attended for more than a week or two. It was just too religious, and the long prayers and praise songs made them quite uncomfortable.

Less than two weeks before Christmas, the met for the last time until after the New Year. The meeting started late. Jane Kime, as usual, played her guitar and led the singing. In the last few weeks, they had sung John's favorite hymns at every meeting: "Amazing Grace" and "Onward Christian Soldiers."

After the singing ended, Chelsea Bue asked, "Have any of you noticed that, except for John, only the original members are here tonight? And apart from Frank, not one of the husbands came."

Only blank looks answered her, so she continued. "I mean, three weeks ago we had almost twenty people here. It was wonderful. Last week there were only ten, and tonight just six. What's going on?"

"I almost didn't come tonight," Marion Nyberg said. "My husband didn't want to come and tried to talk me into staying home with him. If it weren't for this being our last meeting before Christmas, I probably wouldn't be here either. I wonder . . . do you think . . .?" Her eyes were full of tears as she said, "Is this a sign that not only is John dying, but so is this group?"

Big Jake quietly but firmly disagreed. "God has a special purpose for this group. I believe He wanted just the original members here tonight. After all, we started this group, and just maybe it will be our prayers that will bring about the miracles we've been praying for. Not only do I believe God has special plans for Westside Church, but I also think that the city of Pinedale will be involved. And somehow, John is going to be encompassed in all of this."

13

THE BUS STOP

The Christmas countdown on the church marquee proclaimed ten days, but Stanley's thoughts were consumed with John and his impending death. As much as he disliked the thought, Stan knew that he had to see John before he died.

Taking the afternoon off, Stanley drove the eighty miles to Minneapolis and turned into the parking lot at 2:30. He entered the hospital, hoping that John, even in his illness, wouldn't preach to him about Jesus, hell, and damnation again.

Turn around and leave, he kept telling himself. Even if John didn't try to preach to him, it would be uncomfortable seeing him after all that had taken place. And yet, they were friends, weren't they? If he didn't do this, Stan would never forgive himself, and Janet would be upset with him if he took the cowardly way out.

After checking at the main desk, Stan found the elevators and ascended to the tenth floor. Stanley hadn't told

Courtney or Stephanie that he was going to visit John. They would have wanted to come along, and this was definitely something he had to do alone.

How will they handle his death? was another thought running through Stanley's mind. No, he didn't think they would take it very well. John's death would break their hearts. But he also felt that in a few weeks they would forget, as children often do. He took comfort in that.

The elevator door opened, and Stan's thoughts returned to the task at hand. He slowly walked down the corridor until he came to an area that was adorned much differently from the rest of the hospital. They called it a hospice, yet everyone knew it was for those who were near death.

Coming into the hospice was like entering a well-decorated home with curtains on the windows, paintings on the walls, and beautiful furniture throughout. At its center was a large room with a high ceiling and a large, beautifully decorated Christmas tree.

Stan looked over the Christmas tree ornaments and trim, and he grimaced. *What a terrible of time of year to die,* he thought. *Not that there's a good time, of course.*

Like all children, Stanley's daughters loved the Christmas season. But this year, excitement escaped the Geraldson house. Every day, the girls asked how John was doing. Janet and Stan tried to put his approaching death in the best possible light.

John hadn't been to the Geraldson house in more than two years, but the girls did see him in church every Sunday. When they spotted him, they would run up to him for a big hug. Occasionally, they sat with him during the service. "Why doesn't Uncle John sit with you?" they often asked their parents. It was a question that Stan and Janet had a hard time answering.

"Girls," Janet said one day, "your dad and I have a disagreement with John about religion. When you're older, we'll explain it to you. It's important that someday you know the difference between John's religion and ours, but for now, we'll leave it at that."

"Stanley!" A hushed voice called Stanley out of his thoughts. It was Frank Jacobson and his wife, Sandra. As Stan walked with them to one of the sitting areas where Chelsea Bue and Susan Howard of the WPAP Group were praying, Big Jake informed him of John's worsening condition. "Stan, I'm so sorry to have to tell you: John has lapsed into a coma, and the doctors now say that death is but a week or so away. It doesn't look good, but we're still praying for a miracle."

Frank's face was the softest Stan had ever seen it. "I know this is terrible news. You and your family meant a lot to John, and I'm sure he meant a lot to you too."

It was at that juncture that two more of the WPAP Group, returning from the coffee shop, joined them.

Big Jake asked, "Stan, why don't you join us in prayer?" *Oh, no,* Stan thought. But at that moment, a nearby door opened, and John's stepfather walked out. *Thank God,* Stan said to himself. He didn't know how to pray. He just wanted to see John and get out of there.

John's stepfather had only met Stanley once before, yet he recognized Stan and greeted him with a firm handshake and a warm smile. After telling him a short version of how John had tried to convert Janet and himself, Stan told him that he just wanted to tell John how sorry he was about his illness—and about their quarrel. "Also," Stan said, clearing his throat, "I want to tell him that Courtney and Stephanie's hearts are broken, and they are praying very hard for his recovery . . . along with Janet and myself."

John's stepfather listened with a warm understanding in his eyes. When Stan finished, he said, "John is not angry with you. On the contrary, he loves you and your family very much. In fact, he's talked about little else in the last few weeks. He talked about you and Janet and those marvelous girls of yours, and he talked about Big Jake and the Westside Prayer and Praise Group. He prayed for you all several times a day."

John's stepfather explained that a similar "preaching" incident had taken place with him and John's mother, so they could understand how Stanley had reacted. Then he laughed, and his voice softened. "But I have to tell you— after seeing John's great faith in action and talking with Frank Jacobson and some of the women of the WPAP Group, both my wife and I have accepted Jesus as our Lord and Savior." He chuckled. "I guess now we understand the gospel message that John, in his zeal, had such a difficult time getting across to people."

Stanley fidgeted. "Could I see John for a moment?" he asked.

"Yes, of course." John's stepfather escorted Stan into the room from which he had just come. He explained to him again about John's deteriorating condition as they entered a smaller, well-furnished room where John lay dying.

Beside a bed at the far end of the room, a nurse examined John. She looked up as the men drew closer and said, "There's no change." Then she withdrew through a side door.

John's mother rose from her comfortable chair next to the bed and gave Stan a big hug. "Thank you for coming." she said.

Stanley looked over at John, speechless. John had no color. His arms and face, which were all Stan could see, were just skin covering bone. He looked dead already, except for a slight raising and lowering of his chest. Stanley would not have recognized him without seeing .

Stan heard John's mother talking as if through a fog. She said that John's weight was less than ninety pounds now, and he was being fed intravenously, the only medical procedure used to keep him alive. The doctors had recommended a last-ditch effort of extremely high doses of chemotherapy, but John had rejected their advice and said that he was ready to go home to be with the Lord. He was greatly disappointed that his efforts to witness to the lost had been so ineffective. He was so sorry that not one person, other than his parents, had come to know Jesus through his witnessing. And he felt that his Christian life had been a total failure.

John's stepfather and Stanley sat down next to John's mother and exchanged stories of their times with John. All the time, John lay beside them, quietly dying. It seemed so strange for Stan to be talking about John as if he wasn't even there.

Reminiscing with John's parents, Stanley recalled an incident John had shared with him about his time in the Army National Guard.

While stationed at Fort Leonard Wood, Missouri, John and two army buddies, also from the Midwest, were returning to base after a weekend pass. They waited at a bus stop just inside the main gate to get a ride back to their barracks. They stood under a three-sided, roofed building with rain and wind blowing by the open side. A young black couple stopped a few yards from the opening and set their luggage down to wait in the rain. Evidently, they were afraid to enter the bus stop full of white soldiers. After what seemed to be an eternity, but in fact was only a few seconds, John stepped out of the shelter and walked over to the couple. He took their two suitcases, one in each hand. "Come on," he said. "Let's get in out of the rain," and he ushered them under the covering.

John wondered why his friends hadn't acted first, since they were both very religious and extremely dedicated to their churches. John told Stan that he had never told anyone this story before and believed that every one of those men had wanted to do what he did. John hadn't been inside a church, other than for weddings and funerals, in over ten years, yet he had been the one who stepped forward. He felt then that there must be something wrong with religion, but he wasn't sure what it was. As Stan finished the story, another couple entered the room, and Stanley decided that this might be a good time to say good-bye.

14

Death's Door

"Thank you for telling me about the bus stop." John's mother said walking Stanley to the elevator. "It doesn't surprise me that my son would do something like that." Even with his shyness, he was always ready to right a wrong."

She apologized that Stanley hadn't gotten to meet John's brother and sister, who had left the hospital earlier that afternoon for their homes in Milwaukee.

She hesitated and cautiously asked, "If our prayers are not answered for John's healing, would you share the bus-stop story at his funeral?"

"Yes, of course," Stanley replied. "But I'm hoping that your prayers will be answered." And he meant it.

As they reached the elevator, John's mother confided that she hoped John would hold on until after Christmas so as not to spoil everyone's holiday. Stan nodded in agreement. He understood what she was saying. John's death would certainly spoil Christmas for his family and for the

79

congregation at Westside Church. And perhaps, for the city of Pinedale itself. Many people knew John from his days as a raving street preacher, his work in the gift shop, and his time teaching Sunday school. In a funny way, Stanley thought that even those who said they hated John might just miss him.

They hugged and said good-bye. Then Stan entered the elevator, somewhat relieved at being finished with the dreaded task. The feeling didn't last long. As he drove back home to Pinedale, he still felt like something was missing. He had thought his conscience would now be relieved. At least he had *tried* to reconcile with John. But he had no peace.

Christmas lights and wreaths decorating the Minneapolis streetlights drew his thoughts back to what a lousy Christmas this was going to be. Would John make it through Christmas Day? He didn't see how, after seeing him in the hospital looking more dead than alive. Stanley said a quiet prayer as he continued his drive home to Pinedale.

"God, the least you could do is see to it that John holds on until after Christmas." Surprising himself, he choked up as he thought of how swiftly John's life was ending. He'd always known that not everyone would get his seventy or eight years, and yet— "Life just isn't fair, God," he said.

Thoughts of his family further choked him up. John's illness and the events surrounding it had drawn Stanley's family much closer than ever before. He realized how fragile life was and how much he loved his family. Life would not be worth living without them. How lucky he was, Stanley thought, to have such a wonderful wife and two marvelous daughters whom he adored. It seemed amazing to him that he loved their mother more now than when they had first met almost twelve years before.

Stan's mind wandered again, recalling a little incident several months ago. While driving the girls to a birthday party, they had asked how their mother and he met.

"Girls, you've heard this story a million times."

"Please, tell us again, Daddy," Stephanie said.

"Yeah, Daddy. We love this story—please, please," added Courtney.

They especially liked the part about Stan chasing after the car with their mother laughing over his lack of coolness. After telling the story for the umpteenth time, he also told them how much he loved their mother. Their faces lit up with joy.

The next day, they'd told their mother what Stanley had said. When he came home from work that night, Janet had prepared his favorite meal and dressed in her best evening gown. It was a most wonderful night. Stanley grinned wryly to himself as he thought that it must be important for husbands to tell their kids that they love their mother. *How many times can I get away with that before Janet gets wise?*

But even the happy memories couldn't erase the trouble he still felt in his soul. Suddenly, Pinedale seemed very far away. He could hardly wait to get home.

In a smaller, cheerless apartment across town, Vicky Wills hung up the phone. She had been calling every business in town in hopes of picking up a second job, but most places weren't hiring—or else they were closed this close to Christmas. Her boys were sleeping in her bed under heaps of blankets. She was still wearing her winter coat.

Oh God, she prayed. *I need Your help so badly. I don't even know You, so I don't know why You should answer me. I wish I could talk to John. He would tell me how to come to You.*

She hesitated, then dialed another number. She waited nervously while it rang. When a receptionist picked up, Vicky cleared her throat.

"Hello—I-I wanted to speak to a patient—John Nelson?"

The voice softened. "I'm sorry, but that's not possible. Mr. Nelson is in a coma. Would you like me to put you through to his parents?"

"No, no, that won't be necessary," Vicky said. "Thank you."

As she hung up, despair filled her heart. John was her only hope, and it sounded like he would never talk to her again. *What a Christmas,* she thought.

At least she had *a* job, even if it wasn't enough to pay the bills. The rent was overdue, and she knew they would have to leave this apartment soon. She wondered where in the world they would live now. She thought the words again even more bitterly. *What a Christmas.*

15

NO INTERRUPTIONS

"It's just another Christmas."

World-weary words spoken by an exhausted salesclerk as Stanley purchased his last gift and wished the young woman a merry Christmas. He'd seen her around before— what was her name? Oh, yes—Vicky Wills.

He couldn't help but wonder what her life was like. What would cause her to be so depressed at this so-called special time of year? *But, then, they do say psychiatrists' offices are overflowing with patients during the holiday season.*

Stan could see why. During the Christmas season, adversity can become overwhelming. *Most people just don't realize how many lonely and hopeless individuals we come in contact with every day,* he thought.

As he pushed his way back out to the cold, wet street, Stan wondered why he had wished her a merry Christmas to start with. He certainly didn't feel merry. Probably habit, he guessed. Everyone tried to hide his or her true feelings, especially at this time of year. He suspected that if her boss had been there, she would have replied, "And a merry Christmas to you, sir."

Not that he was offended by her response. Quite honestly, Stan agreed with her. This Christmas was going to be rather joyless.

His thoughts were far away as he drove Stephanie to church. They had dropped off Janet and Courtney earlier. It was Christmas Eve. Janet would be rehearsing with the choir, and Courtney was getting into her costume and going over her lines for the Nativity play.

"Daddy, are you listening to me?" Stephanie asked.

"I'm sorry, honey, I guess my mind was a million miles away. What did you say?"

"You missed the turnoff back there."

Stan snapped his attention back to the road. She was right. "Well, ah, I just wanted to show you the Christmas lights at the old Miller place. Anyway, we have plenty of time, sweetheart, before the service starts."

Stephanie sat back and said quietly, "It won't be the same without Uncle John."

Stanley sighed. There had been some talk of his family skipping the usual fellowship time after the service. Every year, everyone brought their special Christmas desserts, cookies, candies, eggnog, hot chocolate, and other holiday beverages. He had tried to persuade Janet that they should just go home. She had convinced Stan that they should at least stay for a short time. Usually they didn't get home from church until after ten on Christmas Eve.

A light snow had fallen most of the day and was supposed to continue throughout the night. Somehow, the snow seemed appropriate. Maybe it would cover up some of the uneasiness that hovered over Westside Community Church this evening.

The latest news on John's condition was that he was failing, and his death was just hours away. Hoping to spare the girls more heartache, Stan had told them that there was no change.

As they entered through the main doors of the church, Stan and Stephanie wished everyone they saw a merry Christmas, but it was difficult to be enthusiastic. It seemed to Stan that the entire town of Pinedale was dispirited because of John's looming death.

Before his illness, the townspeople had avoided him. Now many wondered out loud if what he said so brashly about salvation and heaven and hell were true. Some of the stories circulating around town had almost elevated him to sainthood. The local newspaper stated that crime in the city was down more than fifty percent in the last two months, although they didn't give a reason for it. Bar owners even complained that the volume of clientele was declining. Rumor had it that several "ladies of the evening" had left town because of a lack of business.

Some spoke of "John sightings" (or maybe angel sightings) in the last few weeks. You know those stories where someone gives a hitchhiker a ride, when ordinarily they would never pick up a stranger. And during the short drive, the stranger talks about Jesus and delivers the gospel message and then he is never seen again...that kind of story.

Stan thought the town had gone half-crazy, especially when the two thugs who had beaten John turned up at the police station, confessed to the crime, demanded a Bible, and said they wanted to see a preacher. It didn't take long for rumors to spread. The story went that they were waiting in the alley to rob a drunk they thought was carrying lots of money. All of a sudden, bystanders said they saw a flash of light and heard thumping sounds, followed by sounds of pain and groaning from the alley. In a second or two, the men found themselves in a dumpster. A man with long blonde hair looked in at them with disdain, saying that they were headed for hell and would be there forever unless they trusted and believed that Jesus has saved them from it. Then he disappeared, just like that! *Served them right,* most of the townspeople thought. The drunks swore he was an angel and that the whole thing happened to them because of what they'd done to John.

Although he hated to admit it, Stanley's life was being affected too, and not just by grief. Even his dream had gotten more bizarre: While turning off the lights of Pinedale, he saw human-shaped shadows behind trees and homes. The more he turned off the lights of the town, the more he sensed evil coming closer and closer to him. He wondered why he couldn't stop turning off the lights. And why couldn't he turn the lights *on?* Somehow he feared that his dream had something to do with John and his skepticism about John's new religion. Secretly, he felt—and hoped—that when John died, his dream would end.

He shook his head as he thought over the stories. *They oughta change the name of this town from Pinedale to Wackyville. The townspeople won't even remember John Nelson a few weeks after his funeral. Everything will just go back to the way things were.*

As for Stan, he would never forget John. In some regards, John would always be his best friend, even though he had complicated his life in the last few years. This would be one Christmas he would like to forget, but he knew he never would.

After hanging up their coats, Stephanie and Stan entered the church foyer. It was ten minutes before seven, so they had a few minutes to visit before the service began.

An abundance of greenery, several spruce trees, and genuine evergreen garlands decorated the walls. Two large, highly polished brass horns with a giant red bow hung over the large double doors of the sanctuary.

The children in the Nativity play assembled in the rear of the foyer. Stan and Stephanie went over to see how Courtney felt. After all, she was to be the angel who spoke to the shepherds in the hills near Bethlehem. She looked so beautiful in her angel costume—nothing like the "big guy with the long golden hair" the drunks had described. She admitted to being a little nervous, but assured them that she would remember her lines.

"Daddy, Mom's here," Stephanie said.

The choir had just come up from the basement and was gathering near the main doors to the sanctuary. Stephanie ran over to hug her mom, and Stan left Courtney to join them.

Pastor Whitehearst moved from group to group, trying to encourage everyone with a warm smile, a strong handshake, a few halfhearted hugs, and a cheerful Merry Christmas. Stan wondered if this was all an act to relieve some of the uneasiness of the evening. He would soon find out.

Pastor stopped in front of them and said, "Stanley, John's stepfather called late this afternoon saying that John was still hanging on, although the physicians were saying that it wouldn't be long. The cancer is crushing his lungs, and he can barely breath."

Stan nodded. Apparently, John's physicians were amazed that he was in a coma at all. This was very unusual for this type of cancer; but thankfully, the coma saved John from receiving extensive amounts of medication to cover up the pain. The drugs themselves would likely have taken his life already.

In any case, John's stepfather had told Pastor Whitehearst that no matter what happened now, he would not phone the church again until after the Christmas Eve service.

Pastor said, "I thanked him for his thoughtfulness at such a difficult time. That the service will not be interrupted means a great deal to me and to my congregation. After thanking him and his family, I assured him that they were still in our prayers, and we hung up."

Pastor wiped his forehead with a handkerchief. "Stanley, I am so relieved that I don't need to be concerned about the service being interrupted with the call we all dread. I also wanted to thank you for all you have done during these arduous times. It has been a very trying time for all of us. It would have certainly overwhelmed this beautiful night. It does look like we are going to have a funeral next week, though, doesn't it? Maybe after that we can get back to normal."

After wishing Janet and Stan a joyous season, Pastor moved on to visit with others.

Janet and Stan just looked at each other, not knowing how to respond.

16

A REVELATION WHISPERED

J anet finally changed the subject. "Stan, you better hurry. The pews are almost full. The ushers have started to bring in extra chairs for the back of the sanctuary."

Stephanie and Stanley walked down the center aisle. Stan looked for a place in the back, but Stephanie took his hand and gently pulled him toward the front of the sanctuary where she could get a better view of the Nativity play. They managed to find a couple of places in the third row and squeezed in on the aisle.

As the six-piece orchestra finished a medley of Christmas classics, Pastor Whitehearst entered through the side door and proceeded up two steps to the landing, then two more steps to the altar level. He sat down on the bench in front of the choir loft, which wasn't much of a loft; it was only a few inches higher than the altar platform. The high-backed chair on the left side of the altar, directly behind the pulpit where he usually sat, had been sent out to be reupholstered. For some reason, it hadn't been finished on time for the Christmas Eve service.

The pastor waited for the ushers to remove the orchestra chairs, then stood, which was the cue for the choir to start singing "O Come All Ye Faithful" as they advanced up the center aisle. The choir proceeded up the steps and around and behind Pastor Whitehearst, but Stanley's mind started to drift.

He couldn't stop thinking about the things Pastor had said to him a few minutes before. How could he have been so flippant about John's plight? For all Stan knew, John could be dead right now. His eyes welled up, and he had to force himself to think of something else.

What would be the topic of Pastor's sermon tonight? Would he even mention John? His Christmas Eve sermons were always about seven or eight minutes long and usually a rehash of a former sermon—that the real message of Christmas was about love and fellowship. It was the Christmas season that brought us together, Pastor always said.

As the last choir member sat down, the lights flickered several times and then went off completely. The only lights in the sanctuary were the two candelabras on the altar and the candles on both ends of all the pews. It was eerily beautiful. *What a nice touch to the end of the procession,* he thought. But then he heard considerable whispering around the sanctuary and saw Pastor get up to talk to someone. Stan looked at his watch when the lights came back on. *7:05. Right on time.*

Composed, Pastor nodded, the signal for the children to start the Nativity play. A few glaring silences of forgotten lines plagued certain sheep tenders and wise men. As Courtney who delivered her lines, Stephanie took Stan's hand. She was as nervous as he was for her big sister.

"Do not be afraid; for behold, I bring you good news of a great joy . . ." Courtney's delivered her lines loud and clear and with enthusiasm. Stanley looked up at the choir to see Janet's beaming face. She, too, was pleased.

The Bues's son, Matthew, with his bright red hair and freckles shouted at Mary and Joseph, "We ain't got no room." Everyone laughed and for a few minutes, everyone forgot about John and the uneasiness of the evening.

The Scripture reading took the next slot on the schedule, but Pastor, who should have read, just sat there. *He must be daydreaming again,* Stan thought. What seemed like a minute went by, then another. Finally, Big Jake, who was sitting directly behind Pastor in the choir loft, leaned forward and gently grasped the pastor's shoulder. Startled and clearly embarrassed, Pastor Whitehearst quickly gathered himself together and walked to the lectern to read the Christmas story from the Gospel of Luke. By the time he had finished reading, the children in the play had joined their parents in the pews. Stan lifted Stephanie onto his lap as Courtney joined them.

At this point, the choir and congregation stood singing, "What child is this who lay to rest on Mary's –" The first verse hadn't ended when the pastor and choir let out a big gasp. Pastor's complexion turned pale. Wide eyes focused at the back of the sanctuary. One by one, the entire congregation turned and looked to the back of the sanctuary where a man stood inside the doorway.

No. It can't be! Stanley stepped into the aisle to get a better look.

"Praise the Lord!" someone cried out.

"It's a miracle!" others exclaimed.

"Holy Moses!" yelled another. But most of the congregation just stood there with their mouths and eyes wide open.

Walking down the center aisle, pausing momentarily to shake hands with several people, a robust John, looking healthier than ever, stopped next to the Geraldson pew. Courtney and Stephanie rushed out into the aisle and threw their arms around him. As he knelt down to receive them into his arms, he looked up at Stan and said, "Stan, I've missed you, my friend."

Stan couldn't respond. He was in shock. His mind would not believe what his eyes were seeing. He had just seen John—at death's door!

John told the girls how much he loved them and then said, as he looked directly into their eyes, "Jesus has heard your prayers." He then whispered something in Courtney's ear for several moments and continued up the aisle to the front of the sanctuary. No one stopped him. No one seemed to know *what* to do.

Stephanie bounced with excitement as she returned to her seat, but Courtney looked puzzled, and to some extent, saddened. Stanley wanted to ask her why, but at that moment John reached the front of the sanctuary, walked up the two steps to the landing, and turned toward the congregation. "Everyone," he said, "please be seated."

Pastor Whitehearst started to stand up. Big Jake once again reached forward and placed both of his huge hands on Pastor Whitehearst's shoulders, this time firmly setting him back down. He quietly but confidently said, "Pastor, you're going to sit this one out. God is certainly in our presence tonight." Although Frank turned red with embarrassment at his own boldness, Pastor obeyed.

By the look on Pastor's countenance, the whole congregation knew what he knew. He had lost the battle for the hearts of the congregation. Hushed whispers of awe and wonder at this picture of health filled the sanctuary. Just to have him alive was a miracle, but alive and well could not be fathomed! John's profoundly sad eyes were gone; his deep blue eyes surveyed the congregation now full of warmth and life. Smiling broadly as he waited for everyone to finish their remarks. Finally, they turned their attention to John.

John's voice was hushed, yet strong, and it flowed to every corner of the sanctuary. "Yes," he said, "a miracle has taken place this night, but it is not what it appears."

John stayed silent for several seconds, and then he turned to look at Pastor Whitehearst. "Pastor, I apologize to you and to the members of Westside Church for all the problems and disruptions I've caused over the past few years. Please forgive me."

Pastor Whitehearst nodded with a sheepish smile. Then John turned back to the congregation.

"You all know me as somewhat of a loner. I'm nearly thirty-eight years old and still not married, I have few close friends, and I could never keep a relationship with a girl for more than a few months. I was so lonely and miserable, yet unwilling to take a chance on a long-term relationship. I know now that I was so afraid of someday having that person tell me that they no longer loved me. Without understanding why, I ended every relationship when it got too serious. Before anyone could push me away, I would push them away. That's why, when I accepted Jesus as my Lord and Savior, I became a zealot. You see, Jesus has and always will love me, and He will never leave me. That's a love worth being zealous over. The scars on my face will attest to that."

He chuckled. "Yes, I do admit that my enthusiasm for Jesus was without knowledge or wisdom in the beginning. All I could tell you was that the Lord was coming soon to judge this wicked world, and that you needed to repent of your sins. Most of you didn't take kindly to that, and that was partly my fault. But the word *repent* simply means to turn, to change, to go in another direction. And *sin* is a word that has a repugnant meaning to the world, yet it simply means to miss the mark, or better yet, to fall short of the mark."

Every eye was riveted on John as he continued to explain. Stan thought he noted a glow to John's face. He closed his eyes for a moment, but when he opened them again, no glow appeared.

John continued, "You might ask, what is the mark? The mark of perfection is God! If you are as perfect as God, then you don't need His plan of salvation. But if you're like me, not perfect, then we must use God's plan. Religion won't do it. Coming to church won't do it. Being a 'good person' won't do it because our greatest goodness isn't good enough."

Where did John get this wisdom, this knowledge? Stan sat there thinking. *He is speaking as one with authority, and with a complete knowledge of the Bible.*

John continued, "The final chapter of God's plan of salvation started on that first Christmas almost two thousand years ago, when God sent His only Son into the world to live a sinless life, then to give His life as a substitute for each of us. He took our imperfections and sins to the cross so that we might live—and by 'live,' I mean live with Him forever in His kingdom, and not suffer judgment and eternal punishment.

"Jesus could have called a multitude of angels to rescue Him, but His love for you and me was and is much stronger than the pain He endured on the cross. In the book of Matthew, chapter 7, verses 13 and 14, it reads: 'Enter through the narrow gate, for wide is the gate and broad is the road that leads to destruction and many enter through it. But small is the gate and narrow is the road that leads to life and only a few find it.' I'll say that again—only a few find it.

"Now, this is one of the most frightening verses from the Bible. My prayer this night is that all of you will join me on the narrow road that leads to eternal life with Jesus." John paused, looked out at the congregation, and then began to call the original members of the WPAP Group to him. "Frank and Sandra, will you join me?" he asked. "And Jane . . . Chelsea . . . Marion . . . Susan. Come up here."

Three members of the choir, Big Jake, Sandra, and Jane Kime, all rose and walked around the short brick wall that separated the choir from the altar area, passing in front of a very despairing Pastor Whitehearst. A few moments later, Chelsea Bue, Marion Nyberg, and Susan Howard joined them from the congregation to complete the seven.

John spread out his hand toward them. "Standing before you are seven members of this congregation who love you very much. Theirs is a love so strong, in fact, that it could only come from God. Every one of you knows that the Christmas season is about love, the greatest love story in the history of the world. God loves you so much that He gave His only Son. This gift we call *grace* is free; there is nothing, I repeat, *nothing* you can do to earn it. But what good is any gift if you don't receive it? Jesus's victory over sin and death can be your victory also. Who will come forward now to believe and trust that Jesus alone paid the full price for your sins so that you may receive Jesus into your heart and receive God's free gift of salvation?"

No one moved. Complete silence loomed for several seconds. Then Courtney stepped out into the center aisle, and before Stan could grab hold of her, she ran to the front and flew into John's arms, crying out, "I want Jesus in my heart!"

As John was praying with Courtney, two young teens went forward, followed by several adults. Before long, each of the seven prayed with people to receive Christ.

Stephanie said, "Daddy, I want Jesus, too. Can I go, Daddy?"

"Yes, sweetheart," he replied. "We'll both go." The words left his mouth almost before he could think of what he was saying. But he didn't take them back. He didn't *want* to take them back.

Janet saw Stan and Stephanie go forward, and she joined them in the line in front of John. The three of them knelt in front of John, and he led them in the sinner's prayer. Tears came to John's eyes as he hugged Stephanie and Janet. Then he turned to Stan, and they hugged. Tears of joy ran down their cheeks as John said to Stan, "Will you join us and lead others to Christ?"

In all the excitement, no one noticed a very disheartened and confused Pastor Whitehearst leaving the sanctuary by the side door, except for his wife and son. They met him in the foyer, flustered and concerned about what had happened, but he told them to go home—he would wait in his office until everyone else had left the church. They would talk about it all when he got home.

17

A REVELATION REVEALED

More than one third of the Westside congregation went forward that night. Many others went home confused, some annoyed, and many puzzled, wondering what they had seen. Had the strange service really been of God? And what would happen to Westside Church now? Those who remained were so inspired that they just went around hugging each other. They were all so overjoyed that no one wanted to leave!

Finally, Big Jake suggested, "Why don't we split up into several groups and go Christmas caroling for awhile? It's only eight o'clock. We must make known to the people of Pinedale the miracle that God has brought about here tonight!"

"That's an excellent idea," John interjected. "Would you and Stan take charge? In fact, Frank, you and Stanley, along with others, are going to lead Pinedale out of the darkness." His eyes twinkled, as though he knew some wonderful secret that no one else did. "It will be *you* who will carry on what was started here tonight."

A bright light clicked on in Stan's mind. His dreams—this was what they were all about. *Jesus is the light of the world. And I was trying to shut the lights off and keep Pinedale in the darkness! What a fool I've been.* He wanted to ask John some questions; but before he could get to him, he heard John say, "Now, I'm going to see Pastor Whitehearst for a while. I'll join you later."

As he walked toward Pastor's office, John turned to look back at Stan, smiled, and raised and lowered his right hand as if he were pulling a light cord.

Frank and Stan managed to form four groups of about twenty very inspired and excited Christians. After many of them had filled their pockets with cookies, candies, fudge, and other sweets, they headed out into the streets of Pinedale to see if the miracle would continue while several youth stayed at the church to watch the little children.

Each group headed for its designated area of town, caroling and witnessing and telling of the events of the night.

Some of the people in Stan's group yelled out, "A miracle, a miracle! John Nelson is healed!"

And the miracle continued. Many people asked the carolers into their homes. Many of whom put their faith in Jesus and repented of their sins. Jesus filled their hearts that night. There were even sights of entire families kneeling in the snow. Many of these joined the carolers, and they split into smaller groups again and again. They had been out for an hour and a half when they began talking about returning to the church. That's when Stanley noticed that John had joined them.

"Where did you come from?" he asked.

Before John could answer, another family came out of their house and asked what was happening. As the church people told them the story of John's healing, their enthusiasm returned, and they continued on. Before Stanley lost sight of John, he told Stan to make sure that everyone was back to the church by 10:15. Pastor Whitehearst had an important announcement to make.

When the girls overheard "Uncle John's" instructions to go back to the church, Courtney grabbed Stephanie's hand. "Come on!" she said. "I know a shortcut back to the church."

With all of the activity and commotion, no one noticed the girls leaving the group. It was snowing lightly as they darted off the sidewalk, crossed a football field, and entered the woods.

"Are you sure this is the way?" Stephanie asked.

"Of course," Courtney said. "I play here all the time. The church is just over that way, through the trees a little bit."

Here in the darkness of the woods, the snow began to fall more heavily. Their feet sank down in snowdrifts. The cheery, excited sounds of the carolers had died away, and the woods felt very lonely. A long time seemed to pass, and finally Courtney stopped. It was snowing so hard they could hardly see.

"Do you know where we are?" Stephanie asked, her voice shaking.

"No," Courtney admitted. "I think we're lost."

"I'm scared," Stephanie said.

"I am, too," Courtney told her. She straightened her shoulders. "But Uncle John said that Jesus lives in our hearts now. I'm going to ask Him to help us." She bowed her head, and so did Stephanie. "Dear Jesus, please help us find the church and our family. We're scared."

Suddenly, there was a flash of light, and both girls felt someone grab their wrists. In an instant, they were standing in the yard just behind the church, and golden light was pouring out from inside. The girls looked up. A large man with long, golden hair smiled down at them.

"You're safe now," he said. "John asked me to watch over you two. And God heard your prayers." His eyes twinkled. "You've beaten everybody else here, but you'd better get inside before they realize you're gone!"

When the members of Stan's group reassembled to return to the church, they noticed that John was nowhere to be found. Stan assumed he had returned to the church alone or was with another group. They were all so excited, they couldn't wait to tell the other groups of their success.

Upon their return to Westside Church, Stanley learned that the other groups were just as exhilarated as his was. His girls, who had somehow beaten him back to the church, were glowing with happiness and excitement. Big Jake's carolers, one of the two groups that had gone to the east side of Worth Street, were so worked up that Stanley and others had a hard time getting a word in edgewise.

After talking with Big Jake and the other group leaders, Stan discovered that John had spent time with each of the four groups. They were trying to figure out how he had been able to do that when they were scattered all over town when Pastor Whitehearst came out of his office. His face, ashen. He looked as if all the blood had drained out of his body.

The excited church members fell silent as one by one, they caught sight of the pastor. When they had all quieted and were waiting for him, he said, "I . . . I did not believe in miracles before tonight. When John appeared earlier,

I have to admit that I was more concerned about losing control of the service than I was cognizant of the miracle that stood before me. I left the service humiliated, and I felt that I had become a total failure. And I was angry—I was so angry with John and with all of you for listening to him."

Stanley felt that another miracle might be happening before his eyes. He had never heard Pastor Whitehearst speak so honestly.

Pastor continued, "I could not admit that I might be wrong about how salvation is attained and about my belief that the Bible is mostly legends and myths. While I was in my office, deep in thought, I looked up to see John, standing there, right in front of my desk. I hadn't even heard him come in.

"We talked for about twenty minutes. He informed me that God had chosen me to teach the truth of His Word—for all of His Word is truth. John gave me several Scriptures to read on the inerrancy of the Bible. I looked the Scriptures up and read them out loud, and though I have seen these verses so many times, my heart burned as I read from the Bible. The last thing John said to me before he left was that Jesus loved me, and that if I would read the book of John, chapter 3, I would find the answers I was looking for. Then the phone rang, and I turned to answer it. It was my wife, Ellen. I told her that I was fine and would be home as soon as everyone left the church. I turned to continue my conversation with John, but he was gone."

Pastor swallowed, and everyone saw that tears were glistening in his eyes—tears of joy. "After reading the third chapter of John through several times, I began to understand what it is to be born again. I realized that I had been preaching a lie and John had been preaching the truth. I started to look through my prayer book for an appropriate prayer when I realized that I didn't need that book any longer. After dropping it in the wastebasket, I got down on my knees and actually began to talk to God for the very first time without my prayer book.

"While praying, an insight came to me. It was the statue of Christ in front of Saint Ann's Church. We all see it every time we drive down Davis Avenue—with the Scripture at the base that reads, 'I am the way and the truth and the life.' There is something wrong about that Scripture, I thought. I didn't know what it was, so I looked it up in my Bible. Of course, I do not know if they did this on purpose, but they didn't finish the verse. It's from John, chapter 14, verse 6, and Jesus is talking. The whole verse reads, 'I am the way and the truth and the life. No one comes to the Father except through me.' A lot of us pastors are leaving out the part about Jesus being the only way to our heavenly Father and to His heavenly kingdom.

"Don't you see? We are not saved by the churches we attend, or by a particular religion, or even by our attempts to live godly lives. It is through a personal relationship with Jesus Christ, through the new birth, which we call being born again. Just maybe, we are putting, too much emphasis on Bethlehem when we should be concentrating on the cross of Calvary.

"A few minutes ago, while I was still on my knees in prayer, the phone rang again. This time it was John's stepfather calling from Minneapolis. It seemed that he had been trying to call several members of the WPAP Group over the last two hours. Well, anyway, he finally decided to call here. I had to call the hospital in Minneapolis to confirm it because my mind could not handle one more piece of bewilderment. I do not understand what happened here tonight, and now I am more baffled than ever."

A voice from the back of the foyer cried out, "Pastor, please tell us what happened!"

"Yes, tell us!" said another.

Pastor Whitehearst looked up with eyes that seemed to burn with the truth within him. "Evidently the miracle is much bigger than we thought. I am sorry to tell you," he said, "John died this evening at precisely 7:04."

18

FOUR GIFTS

Stan's family drove home in somber silence that night, except for Stephanie's occasional sobs. Janet held Stephanie in the backseat, while Courtney sat in the front with Stan. Actually, she knelt on the seat, facing the back, telling her little sister how John was all right and that he was with Jesus now. Stan listened—she was saying all the things he and Janet should have been explaining to Stephanie.

He asked Courtney, "Do you understand, sweetheart, that we will never see John again? At least not until we go to heaven someday."

"Daddy," she said confidently, "John told me what was going to happen when he whispered in my ear."

Stan swerved a little but quickly gained control. "What honey? What did he tell you?"

"He said that he had been with Jesus and that Jesus sent him back to tell the people the true meaning of Christmas. Then he was going back to be with Jesus forever."

She continued, "John told me not to tell anyone until after Pastor Whitehearst had made the announcement. He also said that I was supposed to tell Stephanie that he was very happy to be going home to be with Jesus, and that she shouldn't cry. Besides that, he said that when we got home, there would be a special Christmas gift for each of us."

With a deep breath, Courtney added, "And that there would be three very special guests Christmas morning, and that Daddy and Mommy would know what to do."

"Are the Three Kings of Oreo coming to our house?" Stephanie blurted out.

"We don't think so, honey," Janet answered as she and her husband glanced at each other in wonder. They were mystified by all the events of that night, and it seemed that the episode was not over yet.

When they arrived home, the girls voiced in unison, "Hurry, hurry, Daddy!" as Stan unlocked the side door into the kitchen. There, on the kitchen table, lay four magnificent gold ornaments. They looked quite expensive, and on each one was the inscription, "Jesus is the message of Christmas."

Stan slowly picked them up and handed them to his wife and children. On the back of each ornament, their names were engraved, along with the words, "Jesus loves you and so do I. John."

Each of them found a special place on the tree for his or her ornament. "These should be the first ornaments on the tree every year after this," Courtney announced.

Janet and Stan talked to the girls until nearly 11:30, and by the time they were done. Even Stephanie had a fair understanding of the true meaning of Christmas. It wasn't about all the gifts under the tree; it wasn't about the goodwill and brotherhood of the holiday season. And it certainly wasn't about Santa Claus and his eight tiny reindeer. It was about Jesus and about the choice we all have to make.

Janet and Stan shared a teary smile. The excitement of opening gifts on Christmas morning would probably never be the same. Yet, they felt that it was a small price to pay for the truth.

Shortly after midnight, the Geraldsons' phone rang. With a puzzled look at his wife, Stan picked it up.

"Stanley?" the man on the other end said. "This is Mitch Peterson, John Nelson's stepfather. I met you at the hospital the other day."

"Yes, I remember you," Stan said. Janet was watching him, curious.

"Is it true what we've been hearing?" Mitch asked. "Was John seen in town tonight?"

"He sure was!" Stanley said. "He came to our church and led what some called a revival. He was witnessing all over town along with a lot of our church members. I've never seen anything like it. And my family and I have all been saved!"

"That's wonderful," Mitch said. His voice sounded strange. "But Stanley, John died tonight."

"I know," Stan said. "Our pastor told us. I don't understand it."

"Neither do I," Mitch answered. "But I can tell you this: John's body disappeared for three and a half hours after he died. My wife and I stepped out of the room for a few minutes, and when we came back, he was gone. It caused quite the panic here at the hospital!"

"What?"

"Listen I didn't tell Pastor Whitehearst about the body being gone, I guess I felt that there was enough drama going on already and it might just confuse the congregation."

"But his body was found?" Stan asked.

"Three and a half hours later, yup. They found his body in a bed in another room. I sure don't understand it."

"Me neither, Mr. Peterson," Stan said. His eyes were filled with tears again. "All I know is that I praise God for it."

19

NOT JUST ANOTHER CHRISTMAS

Courtney and Stephanie ran into Janet and Stan's bedroom. 7:32 shone bright on the nightstand clock. They rubbed the sleepiness out of their eyes, slipped on their bathrobes, and followed the girls downstairs. The girls were allowed to open one of their gifts this Christmas morning before gathering in the kitchen to have breakfast.

Close to 8:30, the doorbell rang. The girls raced for the door. Janet dashed for the bedroom to get dressed. Stan adjusted his bathrobe and, with high anticipation, followed the girls.

He heard a woman's voice at the entryway and, as he arrived, Stan eyes widened. There stood an attractive young woman who looked to be about twenty-five years old with two of the cutest little boys he had ever seen, none could be older than five. He recognized the woman from somewhere—and then it came to him. She was the salesclerk who had said, "It's just another Christmas."

John was right; Stan knew just what to do.

The young woman introduced herself as Vicky Wills and explained that she lived on the east side of town. She said, "I heard the carolers last night and felt compelled to go outside and talk to them. I never saw so much excitement and enthusiasm on any Christmas Eve. They were calling out that a miracle happened, that John Nelson had been healed."

"Yes, it was a magnificent night."

Her excitement ramped up: "When I walked outside, I met Frank and Sandra Jacobson, who told me about the gospel and led me in the sinner's prayer. They said I become a born-again Christian last night."

"Congratulations, Vicky. That's wonderful news!"

"Then John appeared from nowhere and told me many things about my life. He gave me some money and said that he knew my husband had left me, that there was very little food in the house, and that the rent was overdue. John made me promise to come by your house early this morning with my boys. But I realize this is very strange, and if you'd rather that we just—"

Stan cut her off. "You're expected," he informed her, beaming. "We're very pleased and excited to have you all here for Christmas." He took their coats and ushered them into the kitchen, where Janet joined them. After making introductions, Stan excused himself to get dressed as Janet prepared breakfast for their guests.

After breakfast, they moved to the living room. There, the girls entertained Vicky's sons while Janet and Stan informed her of the events of the last several months.

The doorbell rang again, and Courtney and Stephanie raced for the door.

"Girls," Stan said, "go back and entertain your guests. This is someone I'm expecting."

With a puzzled look from his wife, he headed for the door. A few minutes later, he returned to the living room with a box full of gifts, which he set down in the middle of the room.

"What is this?" asked Janet as the four children gathered around, their eyes wide with anticipation.

Stan's eyes twinkled. "These are gifts for Vicky and her sons, since they are now part of our family."

"I can't possibly accept these," said Vicky. But Janet interrupted her.

"Vicky, God has brought you and your sons to our home. Stan is right: you are part of our family now."

Vicky started to cry, and Janet put her arms around her and held her. The boys immediately came to her side.

"Why is Mommy crying?" the boys wanted to know.

"Sometimes people cry when they're very happy," Stan tried to explain.

Turning to Vicky, he said, "While you were eating breakfast, I made some phone calls and found that many in our church want to help you. In fact, I've learned of several job opportunities. One of the most interesting of those is the offer to manage John's gift shop. Evidently John made this offer known to Big Jake last night. The job would include free rent of the apartment upstairs. We don't want to run your life, Vicky, but I hope you'll let us help wherever we can."

Vicky only nodded, too overwhelmed to say anything. But the hope in her eyes said more than words.

Stan continued, "The gifts are from our family to your family. You know that we Christians help each other from time to time. Someday, there may be a family you can help."

Everyone opened their gifts then. The boys were so excited, they didn't know which toy to play with first!

Courtney and Stephanie were more thrilled with their new friends than they were with their own gifts. They seemed to love these little boys from the moment they saw them.

As the boys played, Courtney jumped up and ran over to Janet and Stan. Her eyes sparkled as she announced, "Isn't this just the best Christmas ever?"

Rising from his chair, Stan excused himself and headed for the kitchen. Janet noticed the glimmer of tears in his eyes and followed him.

"Honey, what's the matter? Why the tears now?" she asked as she sat down next to Stan at the kitchen table.

"I was just thinking how wonderful John looked last night. Yes, the scars were still on his face, but now they're a badge of honor. And those sad eyes—they were gone. John will never be lonely again."

Janet was quiet a moment, and then said, "He made a success of his life after all."

"That he did," Stan replied. He smiled, listening to the sounds of his own changed life floating in from the living room. "That he did."

This book is dedicated to my Lord and Savior Jesus,
The Anointed One,
the God of Abraham, Isaac, and Jacob.

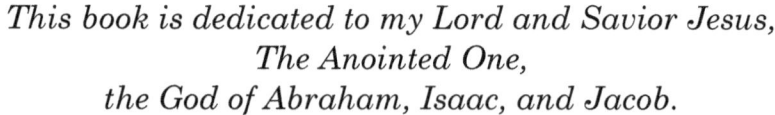

112

EPILOGUE

While *The Pinedale Incident* is fiction, the story behind it is very real. In the early 90s, my doctor discovered a growth on my kidney. As a new Christian, I worried greatly, *If I die, what will Jesus say to me about my first few years as a Christian?* I knew that I certainly hadn't done enough to proclaim the Gospel message.

The next night, a Christian friend asked me to go with him to a healing service—not at my church—but I agreed to go anyway. During that service, a power hit me with great force, like electricity flowing through my body. I truly felt that God was healing me but upon returning home, I was in more pain than ever. On further reflection, I believed that I had experienced God during the service but felt that His answer for my healing was no.

I lay in bed that night thinking about my eventual death and maybe or maybe not being healed. It was during this time of seeking answers that the ending of the *Pinedale Incident* developed in my mind.

The next day at Sunday service, I asked my Christian friend to round up the Prayer and Praise Group from our church and come to my apartment to pray for my healing. They did come. They prayed and anointed me with oil.

Monday morning, I went to the hospital to get a CAT scan. Late that afternoon, the doctor called—the growth was gone! Thank you, God!

I spent the next several months thinking about my ending to *The Pinedale Incident.* One night, I got out of bed at three in the morning and wrote it down, the same ending I thought of after the healing service. That's how the writing process began. Over many years, I added bits and pieces from time to time, with much rethinking and rewriting.

Some readers may be wondering if the ending of the book agrees with Scripture. Certainly, people are healed or brought back to life many times in the Bible. And when healed, they were brought back to perfect health.Some might think John died and his body resurrected during those three and a half missing hours. Whether John is healed or is in his resurrected body you decide. Here are the Scriptures (taken from the New International Version of the Bible) for further reading and discussion: Remember, when Jesus healed someone they were returned to perfect health.

Joel 2:28-30 (The Old Testament Prophet is writing in the name of the Lord. He is describing the signs and events of the coming Day of the Lord, the end of times.)

> I will pour out my Spirit on all people. Your sons and daughters will prophesy, your old men will dream dreams, you young men will see visions. Even on my servants, both men and women, I will pour out my Spirit in those days. I will show wonders in the heavens and on the earth, blood and fire and billows of smoke.

Matthew 27:52-53 (This occurs upon the death of Jesus)

The tombs broke open and the bodies of many holy people who had died were raised to life. They came out of the tombs, and after Jesus' resurrection they went into the holy city and appeared to many people.

John 12:9-10 (This happens after Jesus raised Lazarus from the dead)

Meanwhile a large crowd of Jews found out that Jesus was there and came, not only because of him but also to see Lazarus, whom he had raised from the dead. So the chief priests made plans to kill Lazarus as well, for on account of him many of the Jews were going over to Jesus and putting their faith in him.

Luke 16:27-31 (This is a parable spoken by Jesus about a rich man who mistreated a poor man named Lazarus. Both men died. The rich man went to hell and is begging Abraham to send someone back from heaven to warn his brothers about the reality of hell. Although Abraham denies the request, he doesn't say it's not possible.)

"I beg you, father, send Lazarus to my father's house, for I have five brothers. Let him warn them, so that they will not also come to this place of torment." Abraham replied, "They have Moses and the Prophets; let them listen to them." "No, father Abraham," he said, "but if someone from the dead goes to them, they will repent." He said to him, "If they do not listen to Moses and the Prophets, they will not be convinced even if someone rises from the dead."

Let's continue the discussion. Tell me about your own spiritual journey by contacting me at cdsljn@q.com.

You can purchase copies of this
and other Christian books at

ChristianDiscountShop.com
Amazon.com
BarnesandNoble.com